'Perhaps I can h

'No!' Thea fumb
losing a shoe in
The chair rocked
tions, she yelped
wrist in a firm grip   contact
with tautly-muscle

'It's all right. You're quite safe, I've got you.'
He stepped away lifting her, seemingly effortlessly, with him. 'There you are, perfectly
safe.' Blue eyes quizzed her in a way that
made her feel anything but safe!

Dear Reader

We're only travelling far with one book this month, as Lilian Darcy takes us cruising Bermudan waters in RUNNING AWAY. A MAN OF HONOUR by Caroline Anderson is a deeply moving book, while Jean Evans gives us her first vet book set on Jersey with THE FRAGILE HEART. Elizabeth Harrison gives us a hero with spinal injuries in THE SENIOR PARTNER'S DAUGHTER, all of which makes up a perfectly super month. Do enjoy!

The Editor

Jean Evans was born in Leicester and married shortly before her seventeenth birthday. She has two married daughters and six grandchildren. She gains valuable information and background for her writing from her husband, who is a senior nursing administrator. She now lives in Hampshire, close to the New Forest, and within easy reach of the historic city of Winchester.

Recent titles by the same author:

A DANGEROUS DIAGNOSIS
NO LEASE ON LOVE
ARCTIC STORM

THE FRAGILE HEART

BY
JEAN EVANS

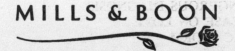

MILLS & BOON

MILLS & BOON LIMITED
ETON HOUSE, 18–24 PARADISE ROAD
RICHMOND, SURREY, TW9 1SR

DID YOU PURCHASE THIS BOOK WITHOUT A COVER?

If you did, you should be aware it is **stolen property** as it was reported
unsold and destroyed by a retailer. Neither the Author nor the publisher
has received any payment for this book.

*All the characters in this book have no existence outside the
imagination of the Author, and have no relation whatsoever to anyone
bearing the same name or names. They are not even distantly inspired
by any individual known or unknown to the Author, and all the
incidents are pure invention.*

*All Rights Reserved. The text of this publication or any part thereof
may not be reproduced or transmitted in any form or by any means,
electronic or mechanical, including photocopying, recording, storage
in an information retrieval system, or otherwise, without the written
permission of the publisher.*

*This book is sold subject to the condition that it shall not, by way of
trade or otherwise, be lent, resold, hired out or otherwise circulated
without the prior consent of the publisher in any form of binding or
cover other than that in which it is published and without a similar
condition including this condition being imposed on the subsequent
purchaser.*

*First published in Great Britain 1994
by Mills & Boon Limited*

© Jean Evans 1994

*Australian copyright 1994   Philippine copyright 1994
This edition 1994*

ISBN 0 263 78592 0

*Set in 10 on 10½ Linotron Times
03-9405-62462*

*Typeset in Great Britain by Centracet, Cambridge
Made and printed in Great Britain*

CHAPTER ONE

An INDIGNANT yowl came from the occupant of the basket Thea Somers placed on the examination table.

'There we are, Mrs Ford.' She smiled at the anxious-looking woman who had just been shown into the treatment room. 'Tibbles is almost as good as new. I'm afraid the operation site is going to look a bit odd for a while. Obviously we had to shave the area on his hip to operate, and you can see the line of stitches, but I promise you, his fur will grow quite quickly and with lots of love and tender care he'll be out enjoying himself in the fields again, hopefully having learned his lesson about not straying too close to busy roads.'

Seventy-year-old Emily Ford's blue eyes filled with tears. 'I don't mind what he looks like. I've got him back, that's what matters. He looked so awful when I brought him in. All that blood. . .' She shuddered. 'I thought he was going to die.'

'Yes, well it was a close thing,' Thea said gently, opening the basket just wide enough to gently stroke the large, black and white cat. 'The car that hit him fractured his hip and Tibbles must have dragged himself quite a way, judging from the state he was in. But we've managed to put him back together and I see no reason why he shouldn't go on for a good few years yet.'

'I can't tell you how grateful I am,' Emily said. 'He's the only company I've got since my Ted died. I don't know what I'd do without Tibbles.'

'I know.' Thea swallowed hard on the sudden lump in her throat. 'Animals are amazingly devoted, aren't they? But then,' she smiled, 'they appreciate a good home and being well looked after.' She closed the basket firmly. 'Tibbles is obviously going to be a bit

5

subdued for a while. That's still the after-effects of the anaesthetic, and he's bound to be in a certain amount of pain, but I can give you some tablets for that.'

'Here we are, Mrs Ford. One, three times a day, crushed up in a little milk and I'm sure they'll go down nicely.'

Thea smiled as her assistant handed over the small packet containing the medication. 'If you can bring Tibbles back in about a week so that I can check the stitches.' Straightening up, she eased her back as her assistant, carrying the basket showed the woman out.

Minutes later, Sandra Watts, the petite blonde veterinary nurse returned to place a cup of coffee on the table. 'I thought you could use this.'

'Oh, you're an angel.' Thea pushed a wayward tendril of auburn hair back from her forehead. 'What a morning! Where did they all come from?'

'I hate to tell you this, but it's not over yet.' Sandra smiled wryly as she began to clear up the discarded instruments. 'We just had a last-minute casualty brought in. It's obviously our morning for cats.'

Thea's grey-green eyes clouded. 'Any idea what the problem is?'

'No, but he certainly doesn't sound too happy.'

'Mm, in that case I'll see him straight away.' Gulping down her coffee, Thea winced as it burned her throat, but she managed a smile as a man walked in carrying a small ginger cat. 'Let's have him on the table, Mr. . .' she glanced at the card Sandra handed to her '. . .Reynolds. What seems to be the problem?'

'I don't know.' He held the animal who sat, straining and mewing pathetically. 'He's been like this since last night. He looks as if he wants to go to the toilet but can't. He won't eat, just sits in his litter box straining.'

'Yes, he certainly looks uncomfortable,' Thea frowned. 'Let's take a look at him. Hello, puss. What's your name, then?'

'Henry.'

'Oh, right. Well, Henry, let's see what we can do for

you, shall we?' Speaking quietly, soothingly, Thea ran
her hands gently over the cat's back, checking for any
possible injuring, then moved to the abdomen. The
animal jerked and tensed. 'All right, puss. Sorry about
this. I won't hurt you any more.' She fondled the
velvety ears and looked at Sam Reynolds. 'He hasn't
been involved in an accident?'

'Not as far as I know.'

'Have you noticed any blood in his urine?'

He frowned. 'I don't think so.'

Thea smiled. 'Don't worry. It's probably not something you'd notice anyway, unless you were specifically
looking for it.' She moved her hand gently over the
cat's abdomen again. 'Mm, the bladder is definitely
distended.'

'What does that mean? Can you do anything about
it? The kids will be devastated if anything happens to
Henry.'

'I can understand that,' Thea smiled. 'And yes, we
can do something about it, though it's a good job you
brought him in as promptly as you did. I have to be
honest, Mr Reynolds, there could be several causes for
what's happening here,' Thea warned. 'It's possible a
tumour could be causing an obstruction.' She frowned.
'I don't think it's as serious as that, but he's obviously
experiencing quite a lot of pain and discomfort and we
need to act quickly. It could be a urinary infection or
stones which have compacted. It's a surprisingly
common condition in male cats.'

'But what causes them?'

'There are several different types of stone. They can
be caused by incorrect diet, insufficient fluid, or by
infection. In Henry's case I'm inclined to think we're
dealing with the latter.'

'But you can treat it?'

'Oh, yes. Ideally we need to make sure that Henry
produces plenty of dilute urine. In this case we're going
to have to insert a catheter into the bladder to relieve
the obstruction fairly quickly. Once we do that I'm sure

you'll see a pretty rapid improvement. Look—' she gathered the cat up, stroking its ears as she handed it to Sandra '—leave Henry with us for twenty-four hours. If you phone the surgery tomorrow I'm sure we'll have some good news for you. I'll be able to give you a progress report and, hopefully, let you know when you can pick him up.'

A relieved Sam Reynolds took his leave minutes later and Thea swabbed the examination table with disinfectant. 'We'd better see to this poor little fellow now. I'll pop the catheter in. What was his temperature?'

Sandra checked the rectal thermometer. 'Just over thirty-eight degrees.'

'Well, that's fine. Let me know if there's any significant change next time you check on him and if you need me I'll come over straight away.'

'Will do,' Sandra gave the smiling reassurance. 'I'll take the cards back to Reception, shall I?'

'Oh, would you?' Having seen the cat safely installed in a cage, Thea finally shed her white coat and was studying her diary when a light tapping came at the door and Andrew Tyler, the senior partner in the veterinary practice, popped his head round.

'Hi. Are you busy or can you spare a few minutes?'

'No, it's fine.' Thea looked up, smiling. 'Come in.' She looked at her watch and grimaced. 'Lor, is that the time? I seem to have got a bit behind hand. Things have been pretty hectic. How about you? Many calls?'

'I just got back.' Forty years old, sandy-haired, good-looking, Andrew chafed his hands before inspecting the half-empty coffee mug. 'Can't say I'm sorry either. The temperature's dropping like a stone out there. Trouble is I've got to go out again.'

'Anything urgent?'

'Could be.' His mouth tightened. 'Jack Dawson called. It sounds as if one of his cows might have picked up some poison.'

'Oh, no. Any idea what sort?'

'He found a half-empty container of antifreeze tossed into one of his fields.'

'Some people are totally irresponsible,' Thea exclaimed, appalled. 'Is it just the one animal that's affected?'

'Jack was still checking the rest of the herd. It was his wife, Molly, who rang. Anyway——' Andrew dug into his pocket for a piece of paper '—I'm going to grab a quick cup of coffee before I dash out, but I wanted to leave you this.' He ran a hand through his hair. 'I hate to do this to you. It's a list of the new supplies that came in this morning. I was going to check through them but I haven't had a minute. . .'

'Leave it with me,' she smiled.

'Oh, and, by the way, those samples came in as well. They're on one of the shelves. Help yourself.' He looked at the clock and grimaced. 'I'd better get going. Let me know how you get on with the samples. I'll be interested in the results, especially that new milk formula. Damn!' He paused in the doorway. 'I knew there was something else. I was going to deliver those bales of straw and boxes of feed over to the refuge for you.'

'Don't worry about it,' Thea said. 'I'll manage. You get your coffee. You look as if you need it.'

Sandra grinned as the door closed. 'Exit whirlwind, stage left. Talking of which, if there's nothing else I'll shut up shop if that's all right with you? Only I promised Mum, next time I had a half-day off I'd take her into town.'

'You go,' Thea smiled. 'I can finish up here. There are a few things I still have to do then I'll lock up as I leave.'

Minutes later, discarding her white coat, Thea wandered into the pharmacy to begin checking a new delivery of vaccines and medical supplies against the list in her hand.

'Right, that's that. Now for the samples.' She gazed at the bewildering array of supplies on the shelves and reached for a chair. Andrew might know exactly where things were, she thought; the trouble was, he'd never quite managed to explain the system to anyone else. 'Ah, well.' Flinging out a hand as the chair rocked precariously, she hitched her straight, tailored skirt slightly above her knees. If she had known her day was going to include this sort of mountaineering act she would have dressed more appropriately. She straightened up gingerly, gasping as the chair rocked.

'If you're thinking of throwing yourself off, I wouldn't recommend it.' A distinctly husky, male voice intruded into the silence, making her jump and the chair rock even more precariously.

Making a frantic grab for the nearest shelf, she twisted round slowly and found herself staring at the tall figure lounging nonchalantly in the doorway. The breath momentarily caught in her throat. It was shock, she told herself, wondering precisely how long he had been standing there watching her struggle.

Blowing a stray wisp of auburn hair from her eyes, she stared down at the intruder. He was tall, around six feet, that much she could judge even from her precarious stance, and a pair of inky blue eyes seemed to be directed unnervingly at her knees. His face was strong, ruggedly chiselled, his hair was dark, almost black, matching the two days of designer stubble on his chin. He looked as if he'd had a hard night and then some, she decided.

But it was a face which sent a secondary shock-wave running through her. Thea frowned. Not classically good-looking, yet there was something compelling about the tanned features, along with something else, something disturbingly unsettling. There was something vaguely familiar about him. Impossible, of course. Thea thrust the thought aside. She had never seen this man before in her life. If she had, she knew she would be unlikely to forget!

She edged one foot unsteadily towards the floor, muttering.

'Not exactly your average, everyday climbing gear, is

it?' he remarked, his gaze lingering with undisguised interest on the length of her nylon-clad leg. 'You're not usually in charge, are you?'

'No I'm not.' Nor was she about to volunteer any information to a total stranger who could be a burglar . . .or anything! 'The surgery's closed.' She tugged at her skirt in an attempt to thwart the blatantly lingering scrutiny. 'How did you get in?'

Powerful shoulders moved beneath the black sweat-shirt. 'I tend to find the door is a pretty safe bet,' he suggested mildly, the glittering gaze narrowing. 'You're not the new assistant by any chance?'

'No, I'm not.' She frowned. 'I could have sworn the door was locked. Damn!' She juggled the boxes she had finally managed to locate.

'You look as if you could do with an extra pair of hands.' A smile tugged at his mouth. 'Perhaps I can help?'

'No!' She fumbled with her foot for the floor, losing a shoe in the process. 'I can manage.' The chair rocked, boxes scattered in all directions, she yelped and his hands caught her waist in a firm grip. Her fingers made contact with tautly muscled arms.

'It's all right. You're quite safe, I've got you.' He stepped away, lifting her seemingly effortlessly with him. For several seconds it seemed she hung suspended in mid-air, then he lowered her slowly, his hands steadying her until her feet found the floor, the top of her head coming to rest somewhere on a level with his chin. 'There we are, perfectly safe.' Blue eyes quizzed her in a way that made her feel anything but safe. 'I suppose you make a habit of this sort of thing?'

A frown etched its way into Thea's brow. 'What?' For some reason her brain didn't seem to be functioning properly.

'You did say the boss wasn't here and you seemed to be under the impression that the door was locked.' The amazingly sensuous mouth moved. 'I don't imagine you'll find many pickings here, but don't stop on my

account.' His voice was pleasantly silky. 'I'm sure
Andrew would be the last to begrudge a few pickings
and who am I to judge?' One dark eyebrow rose. 'If
you tell me what you're looking for maybe I can help?'

The mists clogging her brain cleared. He actually
thought *she* was a burglar! He was laughing at her. 'I
don't believe this is happening,' she snapped edgily.
'Let go of me before I. . .'

'Scream?' He released her but the smile didn't fade
one jot. 'Go ahead if it will make you feel better,
though I doubt anyone's likely to hear. You said
yourself, the place is deserted. . .'

'I said no such thing.' Her mouth snapped to a close
as she recognised the futility of a denial. He was
actually enjoying this, the wretch, Thea thought as she
stepped back firmly but not quite far enough to escape
the subtle, musky fragrance of expensive aftershave.
'Have you been drinking?' She eyed him sharply. Dear
God, being trapped by a burglar was one thing, a
drunken burglar was something else.

'Not yet,' he said easily, 'though I must admit the
idea does have a certain charm.'

'Why exactly are you here?' She chose to ignore his
sarcasm picking up the scattered boxes from the floor
instead. 'The surgery is closed.'

'It isn't important.' He moved away from her, stuffing
his hands in the pockets of a pair of denims which, for
all they were faded, still bore the stamp of a designer
label.

A burglar with expensive tastes—worse and worse.
She groaned inwardly, watching as his gaze flitted lazily
over the well-stacked shelves that adorned the room.

'Maybe I can help,' she said testily.

'It can wait,' he said. 'I thought I might see Andrew.'

'Andrew? You know Andrew?' So why hadn't she
ever seen him around? 'Well, I'm sorry, but he isn't
here. . .at the moment.' She passed her tongue over
dry lips. 'It's a pity you didn't think to warn him you
were coming. You might have saved yourself a trip.'

'It seems like it, doesn't it?' His attention was diverted from a cluttered noticeboard. 'Still the journey wasn't entirely wasted.' He quirked one dark eyebrow at her and Thea felt an odd, fluttering sensation stir somewhere beneath her ribcage.

Indigestion, she told herself firmly, fighting the oddly disturbing feeling that there was something definitely familiar about this man. It was something about those eyes, or maybe it was the voice. Whatever it was the memory was too fragmented. She shook her head and juggled the boxes, wedging one beneath her chin wondering how she was going to fit everything into the small van. More to the point, how was she going to manoeuvre past him in the confined space of the small pharmacy?

'Look, I'm sorry,' she said, 'but I have to lock up.' She hesitated. 'Perhaps I could give Andrew a message?'

'It's not important. I'll catch him again some time. Here, let me take those.'

'No, really, I can manage,' she murmured, stepping back. He gave a howl of pain. 'What's wrong?' She twisted just as his head came up, making sharp contact with the boxes.

He swore softly under his breath. 'My foot,' he said, hopping as he inspected the clear indentation of her three-inch stiletto heel imprinted firmly in his shoe.

'Oh I'm sorry,' Thea chewed at her lip. 'There isn't much room. I did say I could manage.'

His sense of humour seemed to have slipped and she watched uncertainly as he fished out a hanky, wiping a speck of blood from the scratch at his temple.

Thea swallowed hard. 'I. . .don't know you, do I?' she said cautiously. 'Only I get the feeling we've met.'

'Lady, if we had I'd be unlikely to forget.'

The brief hint of savagery in his voice made Thea hesitate. She shuffled the boxes on to the desk. 'It's just that there's something about you. . .'

'What did the last one die of? Multiple injuries?' he

gritted. He hobbled over to half sit on the desk, his jaw moving in a grimace.

'I've said I'm sorry. It was an accident.'

'Sure,' he said grudgingly. 'Take no notice.'

Thea moistened her lips. 'I know it's none of my business. . .'

'Why do I get the impression it's not going to make the slightest difference?' He frowned. 'I don't suppose there's the remotest chance of getting a cup of strong black coffee around here?'

'Try the café down the road,' she said churlishly.

He grunted. 'I'm not sure I can get that far.'

He did look decidedly the worse for wear. Sympathy vied briefly with Thea's natural sense of caution and lost. 'The best cure for a hangover is sleep,' she said bluntly. 'A little food probably wouldn't come amiss either.'

He considered her from beneath thick, dark lashes. 'If that's an invitation, how about lunch?'

Thea choked. 'You must be joking. Besides, have you any idea what time it is?'

He grunted. 'OK, so lunch is out. Dinner then.'

Her mouth tightened. 'I have to go,' she advised him shortly. With jerky movements she rifled through a drawer, scribbled a hasty note for Andrew. 'I'm going to lock up now,' she said decisively. 'Unless you want to spend the weekend here, alone and hungry, I suggest you think seriously about making a move.' She slammed the drawer shut.

He winced. 'Must you do that?'

'Maybe you should stay out of the pub until later in the day, or you could try taking a little water with it.'

His jaw clenched perceptibly. 'Don't give me any aggravation, lady. I've had a hell of a twenty-four hours. I've got a thumping headache and the day is still young.'

'All the more reason to sleep it off,' she said acidly.

He raised one eyebrow. Releasing an exasperated

breath, Thea hunted in her bag, producing a bottle of aspirin. She shook two into her hand.

'Here. With a little luck they may help to sweeten your temper too.'

'And which particular school of charm did you graduate from?'

Thea's chin lifted. 'Don't take your temper out on me,' she said coolly. 'I'd recommend you go and find that coffee and now, if you don't mind, I have to lock up. I should have left here a quarter of an hour ago. I suggest you try the Copper Kettle, on the market square.'

'I'll do that.' He sketched a salute and sauntered to the door. 'I'll see myself out. Oh, and if you see Andrew, tell him I called.'

And how was she supposed to do that? Thea stared abstractedly at the door, when she didn't know him from Adam.

'Wait! I don't know your na. . .' Oh, well, she shrugged. Maybe she had just imagined the feeling of familiarity. He certainly couldn't be local. In a small community like this everyone knew everyone else, and his certainly wasn't the kind of face you'd forget.

She shook herself. Why on earth was she letting it bother her, when she would never see him again? Bracing herself, she collected the boxes and finally locked the door behind her.

Loading them into the van, along with a bale of straw and a large bag of animal feed, she concentrated her thoughts instead, on the chores she still had to do when she got back. Top priority, as always, would be to check and feed the animals.

Without even being aware of it, Thea sighed. Lately it was becoming more and more difficult to keep the refuge going. She had toyed with the idea of a visit to see her bank manager, to see if she could raise a small loan. But at the last minute she had rejected the idea. Getting into debt wouldn't solve the long-term problems.

It wasn't just the cost of feeding the animals, though that was bad enough. There was also the cost of medicines and the constant upkeep of the cages. Oh, it hadn't been too bad in the beginning, but gradually things had begun to get out of hand.

The refuge had started almost as something of a joke. She had taken in a stray cat which had been found injured by the side of the road. Then it had been a fox cub and before she knew it the local children had started bringing in every stray or sick animal until, somehow, things had got out of hand.

She sighed again, juggling the positions of boxes and straw. One rabbit, for instance, was no problem, but when Thumper had promptly proceeded to give birth to five new little Thumpers, things took on a whole new aspect, and it wasn't just a question of raising funds to buy food, space was becoming a problem too.

Luckily she still had six months to run on her lease. But when Bob's successor moved in next door, would he be so obliging about the rent? Or the refuge itself, for that matter?

Thea chewed at her lower lip. Her arrangement with old Dr Craig had been a friendly one. When she had bought into the practice with Andrew three years ago, she had paid what she could for a piece of land Bob Craig had no use for. Maybe it was because he was a doctor that he had understood how she felt. But not everyone had Bob's generosity of spirit, especially when it came to animals, Thea realised.

She climbed in behind the steering-wheel, hunting for her keys. No, a bank loan wasn't the answer, but somehow she was going to have to raise some money and just pray that the new owner wasn't looking to make a huge profit.

Slipping off the handbrake, she put the car into reverse gear and began to ease slowly out of the small space. Perhaps she could appeal to the new owner's better nature, whoever he was, and always assuming he had one, of course. Damn, why did life have to be so complicated?

'Look out!'

The warning shout came too late. A sudden thud sent her jerking forward and she groaned aloud at the sound of breaking glass.

'Oh, no, that's all I need.' Closing her eyes briefly her hand was on the door-handle when someone jerked it open for her.

'You crazy idiot! Oh, my God, not you again. What is it with you, lady? Have you got something against me personally or men in general?'

'You!' Thea snapped, resenting the firm hand which seemed effortlessly to draw her out of the van. 'Don't be so ridiculous.' She was damned if she was going to be browbeaten by some Johnny-come-lately who just happened to drift into town and behaved as if he owned it. Turning on her heel, she marched to the rear of the van and groaned inwardly.

'It's a bit of a mess, isn't it?'

Her brows shot up. 'I don't know why you're so het up when it's my van that took most of the damage.'

'It's rough justice.'

Rough justice indeed! He was gloating. There wasn't a scratch on the dark green Porsche. It had a bright, city look about it, a decadence that seemed out of place in the small, market town, and that rankled too.

'Nice, isn't she?' He patted the bonnet affectionately.

Thea scowled. 'Anyone with half a brain can see there isn't room for two cars to park here.'

'Lady, if I'd known that was yours,' he nodded disparagingly in the direction of her Land Rover, 'nothing would have induced me to park within a five-mile radius.'

She drew in a sharp breath. He really was the most objectionable, arrogant man she had ever met. 'There's no need to be so rude, and stop calling me "lady".'

He smiled thinly, leaning one arm against the car.

'An alternative springs to mind. I'm not sure you'd like it.'

'The name is Somers,' she said tightly. 'Thea Somers. Your temper hasn't improved, I see.'

'My temper was fine until you came along.'

'Don't be so childish.' She glanced, frowning, at her watch. 'Well, as you've sustained no damage I'll be on my way. I have things to do.' Carefully side-stepping his outstretched arm, she opened the door and slid into the driver's seat of the Land Rover. She had to turn the key twice before the ignition fired.

He leaned in through the open window. 'Don't you think we should at least exchange information? Names . . .addresses?' His brows were drawn together in a frown that created a tiny line above his nose. 'I mean, how will I know where to get hold of you? You can call me Joel, by the way. Joel Forrester.'

Thea thrust the car noisily into gear. 'You won't need to get hold of me, Mr Forrester. Oh, and, by the way——' she began vigorously to wind up the window '—did I forget to mention that this is a no-parking zone, unless you happen to be a disc-holder or loading or unloading?'

Her foot was on the accelerator. Out of the corner of her eye she caught a glimpse of the traffic warden advancing purposefully in their direction.

Joel Forrester stepped back sharply. In her rear-view mirror she caught a glimpse of dark fury and mingled frustration on his taut features and chuckled softly to herself.

She had escaped, though precisely from what she wasn't sure. But it had a lot to do with a pair of dark blue eyes that promised retribution.

Out on the open road she put her foot down, putting the miles and him behind her, thankful that she would never see him again. Joel, she mused. Nice name, shame about the man.

CHAPTER TWO

ELEVEN o'clock. Thea peered in drowsy disbelief at the clock. Lulled by the sound of her favourite classical music and the warm glow of the fire, she had almost dozed off on the sofa, and that wouldn't do. She had another full day ahead of her tomorrow and needed all the sleep she could get.

Yawning widely, she straightened her bare legs, stretching as she drained the last of her milky chocolate drink. Fastening the belt of the heavy, towelling robe around her she padded through to the kitchen with her empty cup. One way or another it had been a very long day.

Lifting the latch on the door she stood for a few seconds, gazing up at the dark, star-filled sky, breathing in just the faintest hint of a frost. Tucking her hands into her sleeves, she leaned her head against the door, letting the silence wash over her. A faint smell of the sea drifted to fill her nostrils. Yes, Thea thought, sighing, this end of winter, with the promise of spring, was definitely her favourite time of year.

It was three years since she had first arrived on Jersey to take up the job of junior partner to Andrew in the local veterinary practice, and in all that time she had still never quite got used to the amazingly varied beauty of the island, from its fertile, green countryside, to the beaches with miles of golden sand, or the tiny bays scattered around the coastline.

Thea tucked a stray wisp of hair behind her ear. Even now there were days when she still almost had to pinch herself to realise that she was actually here, doing what she had wanted to do almost from the time she could walk.

A smile tugged at the corners of her generous mouth.

How many people got to fulfil a dream? she wondered. Because that was how it still seemed. Ever since she was a small child, she had loved animals with a kind of devotion which must, at times, have driven her parents to distraction. Where most of her friends had bandaged their dolls, she had practised first aid on the large but, thankfully, docile family Labrador. It had been something of a joke that the garden shed was an extension of the local pet shop, its shelves housing gerbils, hamsters and guinea pigs, not to mention the occasional snake.

From the age of ten, Thea had known she wanted to be a vet, so that, by the time she left school and when most of her friends were heading for office jobs or secretarial courses, no one was surprised when she had headed straight for veterinary college.

Fondling the ears of the collie following at her heels, she turned back to the kitchen. The dog sank into her bed close to the boiler, chin on paws, watching as Thea tidied away cups and unplugged the electric kettle.

'Sleep tight, Jess.' Thea smiled, her hand on the light switch. 'Hope the bugs don't bite.' She turned away and had reached the door when a low rumbling sounded in the collie's throat.

'Come on, Jess, it's too late for games,' Thea pleaded. 'Some of us have to be up in the morning.'

The dog, ears pricked, was out of her bed, pawing at the back door.

'Don't do this to me, Jess. I'm beat.' Thea ran a hand distractedly through her hair. 'Look, it's probably a cat. . .' She broke off, stiffening at the sound of a dull thud coming from somewhere in the dark, followed by a loud cacophony of squawking. 'All right, Jess. I hear it too.' Her hand went down to the dog, silencing the throaty growl. Something, or someone, was out there.

Instinctively her hand went to the light switch, plunging the room into darkness. Edging the door open fractionally, she peered out. Her eyes rapidly adjusting to the change in light, she scanned the yard and paddock.

There was no sign of movement but her cages were out there and she could hear snuffling sounds of protest. 'Oh, no!' Fumbling in a drawer for a torch, she ran into the yard and almost at once her gaze took in the broken fence panel. With a cry of dismay she ran to the old stable which housed the cages in which she kept her animals. Two of the doors were swinging open and even before she reached them she knew they would be empty. But she knew she had locked them securely because she had checked as she did every night when making her final round.

'Why would anyone want to do such a thing?' She looked at the dog at her heels in mute appeal. Then she remembered that Andrew had warned her the previous week that there had been a couple of acts of vandalism in the neighbourhood. Several farm gates had deliberately been left open. There had even been a small barn fire, though luckily it had been spotted in time and no one had been hurt. But this. . .

She looked quickly over the other cages and saw with a surge of relief that the catches were still fastened. 'Good girl, Jess,' she murmured, going down on her haunches beside the collie. 'It looks as if your barking must have disturbed them before they could do any real damage.' But she couldn't leave the missing animals to fend for themselves. Goldie, the young fox cub, had injured its leg and the wound was only just beginning to heal. As for Gerald, with his damaged front paw, he wouldn't stand a chance, not if the local cat was out hunting. Straightening up, she peered into the darkness. The occupants of a nearby hen coop seemed suddenly to have come to life.

Shining the torch ahead of her, Thea scanned the perimeter fence, surrounding the small paddock. One of the panels had been forced aside, leaving a small hole. 'Well at least we know how the culprits got in,' she said softly. 'The question is, are they still around?'

Manoeuvring the wooden section roughly back into place, she glanced across the adjoining field to Bob Craig's old cottage and frowned.

'That's strange. There's a light on.' She felt the breath catch in her throat. Squatters, maybe? Or the same young thugs who had released her animals?

As if sensing her unease, the collie gave another deep-throated growl. Thea reached out to lay a hand on the dog's head, silencing her. 'I know,' she said softly. 'I miss Bob too, but right now we'd better start rounding up the strays, preferably without waking up the entire neighbourhood.'

There was something highly incongruous about chasing over a paddock in the dead of night, wearing slippers and a robe over her nightie, Thea acknowledged as she skirted the cottage and made for the hen coop. It didn't need an expert to tell her that it was the first place her escapees were likely to head for.

On hands and knees she shone the torch beneath the raised, slatted wooden floor of the hut. Two tiny, jewel-like pinpoints of light glowed back at her through the darkness, followed by a hasty scuffling sound.

'Gerald?' she breathed. 'This is no time to be acting up. I know you're in there.' More scuttling. 'Gerald, if you know what's good for you you'll give yourself up.' She swung the beam of the torch. 'You're an ingrate, you know that, Gerald? It would jolly well serve you right if I left you to the cats.' Thea shivered. 'This isn't funny any more, Gerald. I'm tired and it's freezing out here. If you don't give up *now*, that's it. You're dead meat.'

'What the hell is going on here?'

The voice, coming from behind her, brought her upright with a suddenness that sent her head crashing against the wooden overhang.

'Ouch!' Tears of pain pricked at Thea's eyes and she watched with a sharp groan of dismay as the torch flew from her fingers to roll in the grass where the light flickered and, infuriatingly, gave up the ghost. Her hand shot out to retrieve it just as a leather-encased foot kicked it away.

'Oh, no, you don't,' a male voice gritted. 'I warn you, don't make any sudden moves or you may not live to regret it.'

A protest froze on Thea's lips. The voice impinged on her consciousness in a heart-sinkingly familiar way, even as she told herself it wasn't possible.

'You!' She groaned softly. Desperately she thought of escape and knew it would be pure folly to attempt it. He would come after her, there was no doubt in her mind. A blinding beam of light directed full at her made her blink. She raised a hand defensively as the light slowly travelled the length of her, from the tousled mane of her hair, over the softly-clinging robe and down the smooth curve of her legs before it jerked back to her face.

'Well, well. Miss Somers.' Joel Forrester's hand closed on her arm. Instinctively she tried to pull away. The shock waves from that firm touch sent an odd jumble of signals through her nerve-endings. Her insides gave an uneasy little quiver. 'Still up to your old tricks, I see.' Darting mockery laced the words. 'What a versatile creature you are.' The pressure of his fingers on her arm was subtle but still a determined statement of possession.

Thea felt her hackles rise along with her defences. She clutched at the collar of her robe, drawing it together. 'Did you have to come charging in like that?' she demanded fiercely. Dammit, he'd probably well and truly spooked Gerald by now, ruining any chance she might have had of coaxing him back.

She looked pointedly at the restraining hand on her arm and the second time that evening she shivered as those eyes spelled out a warning she would dismiss at her peril.

'You're hurting me.'

She was released instantly. Bending to retrieve her torch she slapped at it in a vain attempt to revive it.

'What the hell is the matter with that thing?'

Thea shook the offending item. 'It must have a loose connection.'

'I'm beginning to think it's not the only thing around here.' The words came hissing out of the darkness.

Her mouth tightened. 'What are you doing here anyway?'

'Isn't that supposed to be my line? As it happens, I just moved into the cottage next door. I was *hoping* to get to bed at a reasonable hour and catch up on some long overdue sleep. Instead of which I heard a commotion, saw a light flashing and decided to investigate.' The beam of light shifted fractionally. 'At risk of seeming to repeat myself, isn't your propensity for breaking and entering getting just a little out of hand?'

'You're right,' Thea said coolly, 'you are repeating yourself and it's still not funny.' She dropped to her knees again to peer under the shed.

'I know I'm probably going to regret this,' his mouth made a hard line, 'but precisely what are you doing scrabbling around on all fours at this time of night?'

'If you must know, I'm looking for Gerald.'

'Gerald?' His brows rose. 'Under the shed?' He snapped his fingers. 'Now why didn't I think of that?'

'He likes it under there.' She wasn't going to let his sarcasm get to her. 'He likes to hide in the dark. It makes him feel safe.'

'Safe!' Came the gritted response. 'Lady, if the poor mutt has any sense at all he'll be miles away by now. What are you, some kind of ultimate deterrent recently unleashed on an unsuspecting world?' A muscle flickered in his jaw. 'Just how old is this. . . Gerald, anyway?'

Thea moistened her lower lip with her tongue. 'Four, maybe five.'

'Five,' he echoed faintly, dropping to his jean-clad knees beside her. 'My God, what sort of mother are you, letting a defenceless kid wander around loose in the middle of the night?'

'Kid!' She jerked up, cracking her head again and let out a yelp of mingled pain and fury. 'For your information, Gerald is a rat.'

'I'm not surprised if he has to put up with the sort of unmitigated violence I've had to suffer today.' Joel Forrester viewed her with distaste. 'The poor little devil's probably going to need psychotherapy for the rest of his life. If I were you, Gerald,' he raised his voice, 'I'd get the hell out of here and not look back.'

Stung, Thea said heatedly, 'I'll overlook the insults because you're obviously feeling out of sorts. . .'

'Out of. . .'

'When I said Gerald was a rat, I mean, Gerald is a *rat*, as in rodent,' she enunciated clearly. 'He was perfectly safe in his cage when I checked an hour ago.' She bit her lip. 'We've had some trouble with vandals lately. They must have got in through a broken fence panel and opened up a couple of the cages. It was probably Jess's barking that scared them off before they could do any more damage.'

Guilt swept in. She'd been meaning to get the fence fixed properly but, as usual, money was a problem and obviously the temporary repair had proved no deterrent at all.

'I'm not so worried about Goldie,' she said and saw his gaze narrow.

'Goldie?'

'She's a fox cub.'

'Of course.'

She chose to ignore the sarcasm. 'She's hand-reared. She'll find her own way back when she's hungry.' She was busy peering under the shed again, calling Gerald's name. 'Gerald has been very ill and it's made him highly nervous.'

'He's not the only one. I've had a long day, lady. I don't need this kind of aggravation. Anyway, no sane person goes crawling on all fours in the dark.'

Well she certainly had to agree with him there. 'Well, don't let me keep you from your bed. Perhaps a good night's sleep will improve your temper. It's hardly Gerald's fault if some young thug decides it's fun to let him take his chances. Anyway,' her gaze rounded on him, 'He's hardly likely to come out while he hears raised voices. I'll manage far better on my own. . .' She broke off as two pinpoints of life gleamed in the darkness. 'Gerald,' she murmured softly, reaching towards him, 'it's all right, you can come out now. The nasty man won't hurt you.'

'Oh, my God, I realise now, this is just a nightmare. I'll wake up, hopefully not less than twenty-four hours from now, to find this is all the result of jet lag. My mind's playing tricks.'

With a tiny hoot of triumph, Thea reached out to scoop the frightened animal into her arms, shielding it protectively. 'He's all right,' she informed Joel happily. 'You're quite safe, Gerald. Oh, look,' she held out the small, furry bundle, 'isn't he cute?'

'I'd rather not,' Joel echoed in faint disgust.

'You're surely not scared of a defenceless little rat?' Thea laughed.

His head came up instantly and she could have sworn he shuddered. 'I've known a few in my life, lady, and they were neither cute nor defenceless. And now, if the evening's entertainment is over,' he snapped, 'I intend going to bed, hopefully to sleep undisturbed for as long as possible. Just do me a favour and keep your rodents under control in future, or I may be obliged to take drastic action. Is that clear? Here.' He thrust the torch at her. 'You'd better take this.'

Thea backed away carefully, cradling Gerald in her arms along with the torch. She may have been prepared to accept tiredness as his excuse for bad temper but referring to Gerald as a rodent with that contemptuous note in his voice. . . The man was too much.

'Don't worry, Mr Forrester, you have my word, nothing would induce us to disturb you again. The place could catch fire but you wouldn't hear a word.'

The sudden glint in his eyes warned she had better get going while the going was good.

She watched him stride away into the darkness, heard the sharp crack of something making contact with an overhanging branch followed by a muffled exclamation of pain.

'Come on, Gerald,' she said soothingly. 'Let's get you safely tucked up, then maybe we can all get some sleep.'

Ten minutes later, having done another round of each of the cages in turn and finding Goldie smugly curled up in a ball, Thea turned out the stable light, gave a jaw-cracking yawn and headed back to the cottage.

In the distance through the trees, a light still showed in the neighbouring property. There was something vaguely comforting about it, after all the weeks it had stood empty since Bob's sudden death.

Thea's heart gave an odd little spasm. She had liked Bob. Not only had he been a damn good doctor, one of the old-fashioned school who actually knew people as well as treated them, but he had shared her concern for the animals she had taken under her wing. Which was the reason he had agreed to lease her the small piece of land.

But it wasn't Bob living there any longer, she reminded herself, putting a vague feeling of depression down to tiredness. It was a stranger, an animal-hating, bad-tempered stranger at that. Presumably Bob's solicitors must have decided to let the property on a temporary basis, until the will could be sorted out.

At least Joel Forrester wouldn't be there for long, she comforted herself with the thought as she turned the door handle and turned it again, and shook it, and pushed. All to no avail.

'Oh no!' She stared in disbelieving horror at the immovable object. But there was no doubt about it, somehow or other she had managed to lock herself out. For a moment tears of frustration filled her eyes before

she dashed them away. This was ridiculous. There had
to be some way of getting into her own home.

But even before she made a check on the windows,
she knew it wasn't going to work. She always made a
point of closing them firmly at night before she went to
bed, not that she was nervous of being alone, she
wasn't. But there were times when she kept veterinary
medical supplies at the cottage, along with syringes,
and she wasn't prepared to run the risk of having them
stolen, so she had purposely had strong window locks
fitted.

Which left the stables or the old barn, with its half-
missing roof. Jess sank to the ground, whining softly as
Thea stared into the darkness, hugging her arms around
her in a self-protective embrace. The night air struck
with a deepening chill. Mid-March, with the threat of
frost, was no time to be sleeping out of doors, she
decided, shuffling her feet. Which left only one alternative. But was she really that brave?

'Take your choice,' she muttered, backing down the
steps to glare up at the tantalisingly darkened window
of her bedroom. 'It's the air-conditioned barn or Mr
Nice Guy. So what's the worst he can do, shoot you?'
She plodded gamely across the paddock. 'Don't put
ideas in his head. The man's already unbalanced.'

Thea took several deep breaths and knocked at the
door just as the light went out. It snapped back on,
making her blink as the door was thrust open.

'What the. . .?' His expression was glacial and this
time she really couldn't blame him. He had shed his
jacket and tie and, in the light, she could see the day's
growth of stubble darkening his jaw. 'What are you,
some kind of sadist?' he growled.

Thea swallowed hard. 'I locked myself out.'

'Great idea.' The door began to close. Her hand shot
out to prevent it.

'Please. . . Look I'm sorry. I didn't mean to disturb
you.' A muscle flickered in his jaw. 'It's freezing out
here. I know Bob always kept a spare key. . .'

He stood very still and she held her breath. 'You make a habit of this?'

'No, no, of course not. It's never happened before. Well, only once,' she added quickly.

Joel Forrester's mouth tightened ominously then he stepped back. 'You'd better come in. I don't suppose you have any idea where this key might be?'

'I'm not sure.'

Sighing heavily he opened a drawer, scattering the contents.

Thea moistened her lips. 'I really am sorry.'

'Save it, lady.' He kneaded at bloodshot eyes. 'I've had one hell of a couple of days. I've flown halfway round the world, missed a flight, lost half my luggage and been set upon by a wildcat female who's a walking disaster area. You won't be surprised to hear I've had about enough for one day.' He opened another drawer, made another futile exploration before slamming it to a close and wincing.

'The dresser, maybe?' Thea swallowed. 'You definitely remind me of someone,' she said cautiously. 'Are you sure we haven't met before?'

'Lady, I don't live that dangerously. If we'd met I wouldn't be likely to forget.'

Thea moistened her lips with the tip of her tongue. 'I realise you've been under a considerable strain and exhaustion might be making you a little edgy, but you have to believe, I didn't do this on purpose. I didn't want to get locked out. I didn't want to get you a parking ticket. . .'

'Well, fancy that,' he bit out, 'and there was I thinking it was all some personal vendetta.'

She chose to ignore the sarcasm. 'At least you'll be pleased to hear that Gerald is safe in his cage and I've checked the rest of the animals and they're all. . .'

His hand froze in mid-movement. 'Wait just one minute. Let me be sure I get this right. You're saying there are *more* of these animals on my land?'

Thea stared at him, uncomfortably aware of a grow-

ing dryness in her mouth. 'Y-*your* land? But it can't. . .
you can't. . .' Now it was her turn to believe this was
some kind of nightmare as horrifying realisation slowly
began to dawn. 'You're not. . .?'

For the first time a glimmer of cynical amusement lit
the dark eyes. 'Bob Craig was my uncle.'

Thea buckled as if the wind had been knocked out of
her. 'Oh, no.' She stared at him. 'At least that explains
why I thought I knew you.' Her brow furrowed. 'But I
thought. . . I seem to remember Bob saying he only
had one relative, a nephew, a doctor. . .out in
Canada. . .'

'I've been out there for the past two years. Before
that I did a year with VSO. I've moved around a bit.'

Thea swallowed hard. 'I'm so sorry. I had no
idea. . .'

He shrugged. 'There's no reason why you should.'

'At least it explains why no one could locate you.'

His dark brows drew together. Seen close to, she
realised, he was younger than she had first imagined,
probably around thirty-five. 'I was away, attending a
medical conference when the news reached me. I came
as quickly as I could.'

She nodded slowly. 'It must have been a terrible
shock. It all happened so quickly. It was a heart attack.
No one even realised he was ill.' Her voice trailed away
as realisation deepened. It also explained the long
flight, his apparent exhaustion. She said resentfully,
'You might have told me.'

'Forewarned is forearmed?' His dark brows rose. 'I
think not. God knows what a fiendish mind like yours
might have dreamed up. Land mines in the paddock,
maybe? And that reminds me——' his mouth tightened
ominously '—just how many of these. . .animals are
we talking about?'

Thea hesitated. 'Not many. Well, possibly quite a
few. But they're all harmless,' she added quickly, 'and
I promise you, I'll make sure they're all kept properly
under control. They won't be any trouble.'

'I hope, for your sake, that's right.'

She shivered, suddenly conscious of her state of undress and the lack of heat in the cottage. Instantly he frowned.

'Key,' he muttered. 'It has to be here somewhere.'

'The kitchen, maybe?'

Dragging a hand through his hair he lifted the latch on the kitchen door and immediately a large, black Labrador ambled unsteadily towards Thea, tail wagging before he flopped breathlessly on to the rug.

'Wellie!' she exclaimed, going down to ruffle the dog's ears, laughing as he licked her face. 'You're back. Oh it's good to see you.'

'I take it you two know each other?'

Blushing, Thea straightened up, patting the dog as he brushed against her. For a few seconds her throat tightened. 'Wellie and I are old friends. I missed him after. . .after Bob died. They went everywhere together. He even took him out in his car when he went on calls.'

Joel gave a wry smile. 'I remember. Wellie always sat in the passenger seat.' He patted the dog's broad back. 'He's slowed down a lot since I last saw him.'

'I'm sure he must miss Bob too. We all do.' Her voice broke a little. 'He was very popular around here.'

Joel gently ordered the dog down. The Labrador sank obediently, tail wagging, into his basket where he lay panting.

Joel frowned. 'Some friends on one of the neighbouring farms took him in. I gather he's been fretting. They thought the sooner he was back on his own territory the better, so I stopped off to collect him on my way here.' He tugged gently at the velvety ears. 'You're not too well, are you, old chap? But then, you must be getting on a bit.'

Thea crouched down beside him. 'He must be at least ten.' She ran an expert hand over the Labrador, who gave a soft hrumph of pleasure but made no attempt to stand. 'Have you any idea what might be wrong?'

Joel shook his head. 'It's just a feeling, instinct. He isn't his old self, but then, as you say, he's probably still missing Bob.'

Thea's hand moved to the dog's chest. 'He does seem a bit warm. Has he eaten anything?' Joel shook his head and she frowned. 'It's possible he may have a bit of an infection. You're right, he doesn't seem quite his old self. I'd like to examine him properly.'

'You? What makes you think you'd be able to diagnose the problem? Oh, wait,' he said with biting scorn, 'don't tell me, you're a witch as well as a troublemaker.'

Mustering her dignity, Thea said sharply, 'I'm a fully qualified vet, Dr Forrester. I gather you know Andrew Tyler—well, I just happen to be his partner. I'm sure if you ask he'll be happy to confirm my professional status.'

Joel quirked an eyebrow as he studied her appearance. His gaze roamed downwards, from the soft tumble of her hair, to her generous mouth, her features devoid of any make-up, and the towelling robe which clung just a shade too tightly. 'You look about eighteen.'

'I'm twenty-six,' Thea jerked upright. 'I need a stethoscope.' Her brow furrowed. 'If only I had my bag with me.'

'I can let you have a stethoscope.' His eyes sparked for an instant. 'I do happen to be a doctor, Miss Somers. I'll get it. Anything else you need?'

'A thermometer?'

He strode away, returning in seconds to hand her the instruments. He knelt beside her as she made her examination. 'Well?' he said, when she sat back at last.

'He certainly has a temperature.' Thea straightened up. 'It's not too bad, but there's a bit of a chest infection bubbling away in there, which would explain why he's listless and off his food.' She fondled the Labrador's greying muzzle. 'In a younger dog it probably wouldn't give too much cause for concern. At Wellie's age. . .'

She looked up to find the blue gaze watching her and, for some reason, it was unnerving. 'Well, as you said, you're a doctor. You don't need me to spell out the risks.'

'But it can be treated.'

'Yes, of course. The treatment is pretty much what you'd presumably prescribe for one of your patients. A light diet, fish or chicken, if he'll eat it. Plenty of fluids, rest and antibiotics. I can let you have a supply first thing in the morning when the surgery opens. You can always take him along and get Andrew to check him over.'

'I think not,' he said softly. He took the stethoscope from her, sliding it into his pocket. 'Wellie's had enough upset lately. He knows you and he obviously likes you. It makes sense that you continue to treat him.'

She was flustered. 'That really isn't necessary. . .'

'It's what I'd prefer.' His voice suddenly had a steely edge to it. 'And now, unless you plan on staying the night, here's your key. I'm going to bed and I should warn you, Miss Somers, there's only one bed, though, of course, I'm perfectly willing to share.'

Thea gave a harsh, choking laugh. 'Don't flatter yourself, Dr Forrester. I'll never be that desperate. I give you my word, I won't bother you again.'

He lifted the latch on the door, took his jacket from a nearby peg, draping it around her shoulders. It still held the warm, male scent of him, of aftershave, woodsmoke.

'Don't make promises you can't keep.' He handed her the torch. 'Sweet dreams, Thea. I'll see you in the morning.'

CHAPTER THREE

SEATED at the kitchen table, Thea ran her gaze briefly over the morning paper, her mind half on the box of cornflakes held poised over her dish. Spotting an item of local interest she read intently, warmed by the shaft of sunlight which streamed in through the window, highlighting the auburn tints of her hair. The sun emphasised the generous contours of her mouth which presently bore a slightly downward curve.

Abandoning her paper, she focused her attention on the small pile of letters beside her plate, yawning widely as she reached for the teapot. Almost as an afterthought she reached to press the button on the answerphone, realising she had forgotten to do so last night. Just as well Andrew was on call.

She buttered a piece of toast as a succession of voices relayed minor messages. 'Hello, Thea, it's Holly Bennett. Sorry I didn't catch you yesterday. Just to say the calf is fine, and thanks for all your help.' Thea smiled. Another job well done. 'Hi, Thea, it's me, Paul. I tried to catch you earlier but you were out. I'm just off to a meeting. Give me a call when you have a minute. Love you.'

'Damn!' A slight frown marred Thea's face as she switched off the machine. She should have checked her messages. Paul Prescott was a doctor who had come to St Bride's just over twelve months ago as junior partner in the practice with Bob, and he and Thea were almost, though not quite, engaged.

She smiled briefly to herself. Somehow they had never quite got round to it. It hadn't seemed necessary. To anyone else she guessed it probably seemed an odd arrangement, but it suited them. One day they would get married. In the meantime she had a busy career, which she loved, and Paul, being Paul, had never actually got around to buying her a ring.

She smiled, wondering what he could have wanted. They had a date for this evening. Maybe something had cropped up and he had to cancel. It happened. They were both used to it, especially since Paul had had to start covering for Bob until some new arrangement could be worked out and, presumably, a locum brought in.

Yawning again, she spooned sugar on to her corn-flakes. The day had hardly begun and already she was feeling cross and out of sorts and she didn't have far to look for the reason. It was alive and well and living the other side of the boundary fence and the prospect of having to go round to the cottage this morning hadn't exactly made for a restful night.

Having Joel Forrester for a neighbour was an unwelcome and unnerving prospect. Her first thought on waking had been how best to avoid him, followed by the undaunting certainty that it wasn't going to be possible. A glance at her watch showed an hour to surgery and already she was dreading it. She stared at her cornflakes and with a sigh of disgust scraped the sodden mess into the bin. She knew she had to pull herself together. A total stranger couldn't be allowed to disrupt her life in this way.

Shrugging herself into a light jacket, she checked the contents of her veterinary bag. Last night Joel Forrester had set out deliberately to provoke her and he had succeeded. The memory of his blatant invitation still sent the hot colour flaring into her cheeks and the worst of it was that, for all the words had been casually spoken, she was certain there had been an underlying seriousness about them, and those feral eyes held a gleaming promise of what was to come if she did! His taut, athletically fit body had sent out signals that had made her blood race and the message had come over loud and clear. He wanted her. He hadn't even bothered to be subtle about it. Joel Forrester was a predator, the worst kind, who swallowed up females — any female, before moving on to the next.

Well, he wasn't going to get the chance. She didn't even know the man, much less like him. With an effort, Thea hauled her mind back to safer ground. There was work to be done. Morning surgeries were always busy and it was Andrew's day to do any calls as well as catching up on routine farm animal injections.

Perhaps it would be best if she got her visit to Joel Forrester's cottage over as soon as she had checked the animals. The sooner it was over and done with, the better. At least then she could get on with her day.

Leaving Jess comfortably settled in the sunny kitchen, she closed the door and made her way to the old stables. Gerald was none the worse for his adventure, she discovered a short time later as she inspected the cages and double-checked the locks.

'And you needn't look so pleased with yourself,' she said in amusement as the young fox cub latched eagerly on to the feeding bottle she held out. 'There are bigger guys than you out there, young fellow. Bigger and a whole lot tougher. Take my word for it, you're better off here until that paw is better.'

Watching him drain the bottle she made a careful inspection of the injured limb. She had found the cub a couple of months ago. Somehow he must have strayed and become entangled in some barbed wire where he had obviously struggled desperately to get free, only to find that the wire had tightened, biting mercilessly into his flesh, so that, by the time Thea had found him quite by chance, he had been weak from pain and lack of food.

Now, a few weeks later, it was good to see the change in him. 'You're doing nicely, young man,' she murmured, fondling the golden coat. 'A few more days of square meals and you should be able to fend for yourself. Maybe you'll even be able to find your brothers and sisters.'

Barney was a different customer altogether. The owl

was obviously no youngster and his wing had been so badly damaged that he would never fly again. Even so, he seemed happy enough and Thea hadn't the heart to leave him to take his chances.

'Go back to sleep.' She gently smoothed the paler chest feathers, smiling as the bird swivelled its head to gaze at her with large, solemn eyes before blinking and turning away. 'I know the feeling,' she laughed wryly. 'Some days are just like that.'

It took about half an hour to check all the animals, making sure they each had fresh food and water, and she realised with a pang of regret that she could no longer postpone her visit to Joel Forrester.

She stacked away the remains of a bag of straw and was washing her hands when the stable door swung open.

'Now that's what I like to see, the peasants at toil.' A male voice chuckled familiarly in her ear. 'I called at the cottage but it was all locked up. I'm beginning to get the distinct impression, Miss Somers, that you are playing hard to get.'

Thea frowned abstractedly at the row of cages before closing the outer door and wondered, fleetingly, whether Paul would actually notice if she weren't always seemingly just at the end of the phone or available whenever he chose to drop in.

'Oh, Paul, I'm sorry. I did get your message but it was too late to call you. Don't tell me.' She smiled. 'You can't make it tonight.'

The twinge of disappointment she felt at the prospect of their plans being cancelled was only momentary. They were both in the sort of job that demanded something beyond the usual nine-to-five type of commitment. He was tall and blond and she smiled sympathetically up at him. 'Oh, well, it can't be helped. In fact I'll quite enjoy a quiet evening in for a change.'

He looked slightly hurt. 'Oh I can make it. I may just be a bit late picking you up, that's all. Anyway, I can hardly let the darts team down, can I?'

She wondered with a brief and totally irrational flash of resentment how he would react if, just for once, she said she had made other plans, then told herself she was being ridiculous. 'Of course not.' She smiled, brushing wisps of straw from her jeans. 'If you're sure.'

'Absolutely. In any case, I wouldn't pass up a chance to see your smiling face. It's what keeps me going. Oh, and by the way, I don't suppose we could take your car, could we? only mine's in the garage for a spot of major surgery from the sound of things. I'm just praying it's not terminal.'

'Honestly, Paul,' Thea gave a sigh of mingled laughter and exasperation. 'Don't you think it's time you did something about that awful old heap.'

'Old heap!' His tanned features assumed a pained expression. 'I'll have you know that car is almost a collector's item.'

She had to laugh. 'The only collector it's likely to see is when the local refuse disposal unit call to take it to the nearest dump. When are you going to get yourself some respectable transport?'

'When I'm rich and successful.' He pulled her towards him, planting a kiss on her nose. 'Then I'll order the Porsche.'

'You're incorrigible.' She detached herself firmly, to slam the door of the Land Rover.

'I know,' he grinned, 'but I'm gorgeous with it and I love you.'

For once she felt too tired to respond to the teasing note in his voice. 'Look, Paul, I have to make a house call before I take morning surgery.' She glanced at her watch, her eyes widening briefly. 'Talking of which, aren't you running a bit late yourself? I thought surgery started at nine o'clock?'

'I'll be there,' he laughed. 'Anyway, I doubt the patients will run away.' His blond hair shimmered in the bright, morning sunlight. He was a good-looking man, Thea realised, and she was very fond of him. But at thirty years old he had a casual, laid-back attitude to life that made her wonder sometimes if he was ever going to grow up, if their relationship was ever going to progress beyond its present stage.

She shook her head. It was too early in the morning to get involved in those kind of thoughts and, for the moment, she had her own job to worry about.

Shading her eyes, she glanced in the direction of the neighbouring cottage and reached resignedly for her bag. 'I have to take a look at Wellie, Bob's old Labrador. He's not too well. I'm just going to walk round there now.'

'In that case I'll walk with you. It's on my way.' Paul fell into a long-legged stride beside her. 'I thought the Wallises had taken him in until some distant relative of Bob's turned up.'

'Yes, they did,' Thea nodded, 'and he has — turned up, I mean. Yesterday, as a matter of fact.'

'Oh, well, better late than never I suppose. Come to rake over the pickings, has he? Nothing like getting here too late for the event, is there? What's he like?'

There was a faintly sneering note in his voice which Thea tried to ignore. 'I don't really know what he's like but I imagine he could be a tyrant to work for. I gather he's been working abroad for the last few years. He was at some sort of convention when Bob died, which is why he didn't get the news in time, but he got here as quickly as he could.'

Paul gave her a sidelong glance. 'You don't seem to have wasted any time getting to know him. I thought you said he only arrived yesterday.'

Thea felt the colour burn into her cheeks. 'Yes, well, as it happens I met him quite by chance.' She gave a slight laugh. 'It was quite ridiculous. I somehow managed to lock myself out of the cottage and was facing up to spending a night in the stable; then I suddenly remembered that Bob always kept a spare key.'

'That was convenient.' An unfamiliar aggression roughened his voice and Thea stifled a tiny feeling of resentment.

'Yes, wasn't it?' She sighed. She didn't want to argue with Paul, especially when she couldn't even pinpoint exactly what it was they were suddenly arguing about. She smiled. 'I should get another key cut. I've been meaning to and never quite got around to it. I don't suppose he'll be here long enough to come to the rescue again. He doesn't look the sort who stays in one place too long.' He looked more the kind of restless spirit who kept moving and who probably had a woman waiting wherever he chose to hang his metaphorical hat, she thought, uncharitably.

'So why the visit this morning?'

'I told you, Wellie. . .'

'So why can't he take the animal along to the surgery like everyone else.'

His dismissive reference to Wellie jarred slightly, then she told herself she was being over-sensitive. It seemed that was the effect Joel Forrester seemed to have on her. She said, 'He's getting on a bit and I don't want him moved around any more than is absolutely necessary. Anyway, Wellie knows me so it makes sense for me to treat him.'

She broke off, pausing at the gate leading to the cottage, A figure caught her eye. For a second she thought it was the gardener, a local man who still came in occasionally to keep the grass cut and the gardens in order, and he did a good job too, if the riot of colour that met her eyes was anything to go by. But the figure straightened, instantly shattering the illusion, and she felt her heart give an irrational lurch.

The faded denims he was wearing were moulded to his thighs. He had discarded his sweater and his shirt was open, giving her a glimpse of the sensuous power of his body as the muscles flexed, shining with sweat.

Negligently, Joel dug the spade he had been using into the ground and came towards her. There was an aura of masculinity about him that took her breath away. He still looked tired, but he had shaved, his square-cut jaw was firm, the hard angles of his face somehow different this morning, making him somehow, subtly, even more dangerous and attractive.

The cool blue gaze swept over Paul before coming to rest on herself. 'I wasn't sure what time you'd be here.'

'I thought I'd get it over with, before I start surgery. I. . . I was afraid I might be too early.'

'It would take something quite exceptional to keep me in bed,' The blue eyes glinted. 'But then, you don't know me that well yet, do you, Miss Somers?'

Thea almost choked. The man was insufferable but she refused to rise to his bait. 'Paul, I don't believe you've met Dr Forrester. Dr Forrester, Paul Prescott. Paul joined Bob's practice just over a year ago.'

'Is that so?' Joel reached out a tanned, muscular arm to shake Paul's hand and Thea found herself staring with fascination at the lighter hairs on his arm. She asserted, 'Paul has been holding the fort single-handed since your uncle died.'

'Really?' Joel's mouth became a hard line as his glance swept Paul before returning to Thea. 'That's funny, I was under the impression that my uncle always started surgery promptly at nine. It's old-fashioned, I know, but he always believed if the patients could get there on time, he owed them the same courtesy.' His gaze returned to Paul, who was now a shade paler. 'Or possibly you've made some changes since I was here last?'

'No.' Paul began uncomfortably. 'No changes. I just happen to be running a little late. . .'

'In that case don't let us keep you.' Joel's voice was low and evenly modulated. 'By the way, I shall be over myself later. Just to take a look round, familiarise myself with the layout. It's been some time since I was last there.'

'Er. . .look around?' Paul shifted uncomfortably.

'Yes. Oh, didn't I say?' Joel's brows rose. 'Obviously there are things we need to discuss, before I take over the practice.'

Paul gasped. He looked as if he had been pole-axed,

disbelief etched into his features, and Thea could understand why. 'T-take over? You mean. . .as senior partner? But I thought. . .'

'Right.' Joel was intent on cleaning the soil from his shoe. 'Clearly the practice is too large to be run single-handed. It was always my uncle's intention that I should take over from him when he eventually retired. I assumed he would have discussed it with you.' The blue eyes narrowed briefly. 'Naturally I'd hoped he would be around to enjoy a long retirement. Sadly that isn't to be the case, but it's all the more reason why I intend keeping my promise to him.' His smile didn't quite reach his eyes. 'I suggest you keep yourself free for a meeting. Shall we say some time after morning surgery?'

Paul was visibly shaken. '*This* morning's surgery?'

'No time like the present, I always say.'

With a tight-lipped glance in Thea's direction, Paul sped away. To Joel, Thea said resentfully, 'Was that really necessary?' She faced him with irritation. 'Did you need to be quite so high-handed? Making your announcement out of the blue like that, without any hint or warning?'

'Would you have preferred it if I'd simply turned up at the surgery?' he queried dismissively.

'It might have been a little kinder,' she retorted hotly, 'instead of making Paul feel. . .inadequate. He's been doing his best under very difficult circumstances, and your arrival must have come as quite a shock.'

'I can't speak for your boyfriend's. . .inadequacies, Miss Somers.' His blue gaze narrowed. 'I take it he is a boyfriend?' Thea stiffened defensively but he didn't give her an opportunity to speak. 'The fact is that I'm here, and the sooner everyone gets used to the idea, the better.' He pushed open the door. 'You'd better come in.'

The phrase 'said the spider to the fly' sprang to mind and was instantly banished as Thea followed him into the kitchen, with its large, solid pine table.

'I was just about to have some coffee.' He took a couple of china mugs from a shelf and reached for the pot. 'Would you like some?'

She shuddered. 'I'm a tea person myself.'

'Coffee's a habit I acquired abroad.'

It did smell good and she hadn't actually eaten her breakfast. 'Perhaps I'll try it.'

'Sit down.' He handed her a mug. 'I take mine black but there's milk and sugar.'

He remained standing, one hand enveloping the mug. 'I'm afraid I don't eat breakfast, but if you. . .'

'No! Thank you.' She got to her feet, feeling a rush of colour invade her cheeks as his gaze swept over her, taking in the figure-hugging jeans and the soft, grey check shirt which had seemed so practical yet now only seemed to emphasise her curves.

Looking pointedly at her watch she said briskly, 'I'm afraid I don't have time for a social visit, Dr Forrester. Surgery starts in just under half an hour. Perhaps I can take a look at Wellie. How is he this morning?'

'He was sleeping when I last looked so I left him to it. I moved his bed into the sitting-room, in front of the fire.'

She let him go ahead of her to where the Labrador lay, curled up in his basket. He made no move to greet her as she knelt beside him.

'Hello, old thing. How are you feeling today?' Her professional gaze took in the dull coat and she bit her lower lip. 'Mm, well, he's certainly no better. In fact, if anything, I'd say he's slightly worse.'

'I was afraid you were going to say that.' Joel came down beside her, his eyes darkening.

Seen close to, he still looked tired. Her gaze went to the armchair. The cushions were untidy. An empty glass stood on the nearby coffee-table.

Thea gave him a sidelong glance. 'Did you actually get any sleep last night?'

'Not a lot.' Humour briefly flickered in his eyes.

'Wellie seemed restless. I thought he might be happier if someone was around.'

'You must be exhausted.'

'I can manage on surprisingly little sleep.'

She could believe it. There was a restlessness about him that reminded her of a wild animal.

Swallowing hard she reached for her bag. 'I'd better examine him.' Wellie made no protest as she checked his temperature, nor when she applied the stethoscope to his chest. Examination complete, she straightened up.

'How is he?'

'Not good, I'm afraid. But then, I imagine you know that.'

'I had a pretty good idea.' He raked a hand through his hair. 'So what happens now?'

'I brought a course of antibiotics with me. Start him on them straight away. Don't encourage him to play, in fact you should remove any temptation in the way of toys. The last thing he needs right now is to exert himself any more than necessary. Not that I imagine he'll want to for a while.' She snapped the locks on her bag. 'I'll need to see him again in a couple of days.' She was already moving towards the door. 'Bring him to the surgery, or give me a call if you're worried.'

'I appreciate what you've done.'

'It's my job.'

'Even so.' He paused, his hand on her arm. 'Look, we didn't exactly get off to a good start yesterday.'

Thea gave a slight laugh. 'I'd say that's probably the understatement of the year.'

Joel followed her to the door. Outside, the promise of an early spring day was being fulfilled and she couldn't resist standing breathing in the air, so unlike that of the busy Midlands town where she had done her training.

Her throat tightened. 'This time of year always reminds me of Bob. He and Wellie used to walk for miles. It's the sort of weather they loved. . .' She broke off. 'They were very close.' She looked up at him. 'Maybe Wellie's just giving up.'

He frowned. 'You really believe that?'

Thea shrugged. 'I've seen it happen. Old people can become very attached to their pets and vice versa. Surely, as a doctor, you must have seen it happen?'

'I wasn't decrying your theory,' he said quietly. 'I happen to subscribe to it myself.'

'Y-you do?'

His blue eyes glinted with humour then he sobered again. 'You thought a lot of my uncle, didn't you?'

She nodded. 'He was a good friend. I miss him. Everyone around here does.' She brushed back a stray tendril of hair and looked up at him. 'Bob Craig wasn't just a good doctor. People weren't just patients to him. He knew everyone personally, by name.'

'If you're trying to tell me that he's going to be a hard act to follow, I'm already aware of that,' he said softly.

She glanced up at the attractive planes of his face. His mouth was nerve-shatteringly sensual. She drew herself up sharply. 'I wasn't trying to score points, Doctor.' She had reached the gate and was struggling to open it when his hand closed over hers.

'The name's Joel. Here, let me.' Blue eyes regarded her with a hint of amusement. 'Since it looks as if we're going to be neighbours, I think we could drop the formality, don't you?'

Thea moistened her lower lip with her tongue. 'You were serious then? About taking over the practice, I mean?'

'It wasn't a sudden aberration, if that's what you mean.' His dark brows drew together. 'Things have just happened sooner and in a different way to what we'd planned. I'm sorry if my uncle didn't get around to discussing things with Dr Prescott, but I made a promise to my uncle and I intend to keep it.'

Thea nodded. Slowly she said, 'I can understand that. When. . .when do you plan to start taking surgeries?'

'I think the sooner, the better, don't you? Under the circumstances.'

Faint colour stung her cheeks at the obvious implication. 'Paul has been doing his best,' she challenged hotly. 'It hasn't been easy for him, especially when people still think of him as a relative newcomer.' She chewed at her lower lip. 'I think Paul always hoped that, maybe, one day, Bob would hand over the practice to him. Bob had been finding things a bit hard going for the past year or so. Not that he would admit it, of course, but I know he found the night and emergency calls less easy to cope with. It helped, having Paul there.'

'I admire your loyalty,' his lips twisted. 'Even if it is a little misplaced.'

'That's unfair.' She turned to fling the challenge, feeling her breath catch sharply in her throat as she collided with his powerfully male body. Her lips parted on a gasp as he reached out to steady her, bringing her close, so close that her nostrils were invaded by the fresh, clean musky smell of him.

The sensuous mouth was only a breath away. Shock briefly widened her eyes as, almost negligently, his finger traced the curve of her cheek before he bent his head swiftly to kiss her firmly on her mouth.

She stood mesmerised, stunned by the power of the sensations that coursed through her. His eyes really were incredibly dark blue. She stared at the thick lashes then, suddenly, she was struggling furiously to break free. What on earth was she thinking of? She didn't even like the man. Worse than that, she didn't trust him.

'How dare you?' She pushed him firmly away.

His blue eyes glinted. 'Just being neighbourly.'

'Neighbourly! Some people might say that was downright taking advantage, Dr Forrester.' She gathered up her bag, and put herself firmly on the other side of the gate.

An odd sound which might have been a cough or

could have been a chuckle followed her up the path. She didn't stop to find out. The Joel Forresters of this world were restless spirits. Here today, gone tomorrow. Well she preferred her life the way it was, thank you very much. Quiet, uncomplicated and totally predictable.

CHAPTER FOUR

WEEKENDS should be longer, Thea thought, as she parked the Land Rover neatly in the car park behind the veterinary practice.

Forty-eight hours of trying to avoid any contact with her new neighbour had proved more wearing than she would have believed possible, especially when it seemed she only had to step outside her door to check on or feed the animals and he was there, digging the garden, or trimming a hedge.

Blast the man, she thought with rare irritation, scuttling away from the glimpse of bronzed arms and male chest, and promptly drawing the kitchen curtains. It was hardly any wonder she felt exhausted. It was a relief to get back to work, and to know that the source of her torment was similarly occupied.

Pausing for a moment, she shaded her eyes and gazed out at the small harbour, experiencing the same delight at the scene now as she had three years ago when she had first arrived on Jersey.

A couple of days of good weather had brought a swarm of early tourists. That was one of the things she loved about the Channel Island. It had something to offer at any time of the year. Beyond the sea wall, the tide was out, leaving a few small craft moored on the sand-bed in the harbour, and even now a few hardy tourists were clambering up a nearby hill to the church, built over a hundred years ago to provide services for the local fishermen and the women who packed the catch.

Turning back to the Land Rover, Thea hauled her bag from the passenger seat, slammed the door and locked it before making her way to the back door of the small but busy practice.

Once inside, a steady hum of noise interspersed with an occasional bark from the adjoining waiting-room told her that they were in for their usual busy Monday morning.

'Hi.' Karen, the receptionist and general Girl Friday, greeted her arrival with her usual cheeriness. 'Have a good weekend? Morning, Mrs Duncan, take a seat. Mr Tyler will see you in a minute.'

'Quiet, but nice,' Thea sifted through the morning mail.

A connecting door opened and Andrew, wearing jeans and a heavy sweater, collected a bundle of cards from the desk. 'Morning, Thea. Nice weekend?'

'Lovely, thanks.' Gritting her teeth on a smile, she reached for a list, scanning the details. 'Are these mine?'

'Every last one.' Karen grinned. 'It's like Waterloo Station out there, but nothing too drastic, I don't think.'

'Touch wood before you say that.' This time, Thea's smile was genuine as she picked up her own patients' cards before following Andrew through to the consulting-room. 'How was your weekend?'

'The usual. Too much to do and not enough time to do it.' He tossed a pile of mainly buff envelopes on to the desk. 'More paperwork and forms to fill in. I'll get round to it later.'

'I know the feeling,' Thea perched on the edge of the well-worn desk. 'Did you get many calls over the weekend?'

'A few. Nothing unexpected, thank goodness.'

'How's Jack Dawson's cow?'

'I think she'll make it,' Andrew frowned. 'None of the rest of the herd seems to have picked up any of the poison, thank God. Jack and his wife have had a tough time of it this past couple of years, since his dad died and he had to take over. The last thing they need now is to start losing the stock. It took time to build up that herd.'

Thea nodded sympathetically. 'I don't suppose they know who was responsible for dumping the antifreeze?'

'Fat chance.' Andrew half sat, half leaned against the table, 'Though I doubt it was anyone local. They have too much respect for the countryside. Unfortunately you'll always get the odd person who doesn't share that sense of responsibility.'

Thea nodded agreement, frowning as she straightened up. 'I'd better get going.'

'Oh, by the way ——' Andrew's voice made her pause at the door ' — Bob's nephew is back.'

She felt her heart give a slight lurch. 'Yes. Er — look, I'm sorry, I should have told you. He came into the surgery on Friday, just after you left. He was looking for you but didn't leave a message.'

'Don't worry about it.' Andrew grinned. 'He came over to the cottage. We spent the weekend catching up on old times.'

'You. . .know each other quite well, then?'

'You could say,' he enthused. 'Joel and I go back a long way. In fact we practically grew up together. He spent most of his holidays with old Bob.'

She managed to keep her voice very cool. 'His parents glad of a rest, were they?'

Andrew frowned. 'Actually they were killed in a car crash. He was about twelve at the time. I seem to recall that Joel was farmed out to various relatives, but he spent most of the school holidays with Bob.' He gave a slight smile. 'I loved it, naturally, having company more or less my own age. We went everywhere together, until we both went our separate ways, me to veterinary college, Joel to medical school.' He straightened up. 'It was great, catching up on old times.'

Thea's mind was still struggling to imagine what it must have been like for that dark-haired, dark-eyed boy, not only to have lost his parents, but to be shunted from one relative to another at an age when any child is at its most vulnerable. She swallowed hard on the sudden tightness in her throat. 'Yes, I'm sure it must be.'

'I offered to introduce you——' brown eyes glanced speculatively in her direction '—but I gather you've already managed to become acquainted.'

Colour flared defensively in her cheeks. 'If there's any question of a complaint. . .' Wasn't that just typical of the man, to go sneaking behind her back.

'Complaint? What makes you think there might be?'

Thea shifted uneasily. 'Well, I. . .'

'On the contrary,' Andrew smiled. 'In fact I gather Joel was pretty impressed with the way you handled Wellie. So much so that he's keen for you to carry on.'

I'll bet he is. Thea ground her teeth together. 'Yes, well,' she smiled, 'duty calls. I may see you later.'

'By the way,' Andrew's voice halted her again. 'Joanne and I have got a tenth wedding anniversary coming up fairly soon. Joanne's organising a bit of a do and I've been given strict orders to make sure you come. Paul's invited too, obviously. Nothing too formal—food, drinks, a few close friends.'

Thea relaxed, feeling she was on safer ground. 'We wouldn't miss it for anything. Thank Joanne and tell her we'd love to come.'

'Good.' Andrew rubbed his hands together. 'It'll be an ideal opportunity for everyone to meet on a social level,' he grinned, 'and I've been given strict instructions that there's to be no shop talk.'

'We shall look forward to it.' Smiling, she made her way to the consulting-room.

A typical Monday morning got under way as Sandra ushered in the first client and lifted the patient, a young spaniel bitch, on to the examination table. 'This is Cindy and Mrs Bailey.' Smiling she handed Thea the card.

'Hello, Cindy.' As always, Thea approached the animal, speaking slowly, while at the same time making a quick, professional assessment. 'She looks in excellent condition, Mrs Bailey. A nice shiny coat, bright eyes,'

Thea smiled. 'A bit of a change since you first found her. I seem to remember she was in a very sorry state.'

'I'll never understand how anyone can ill-treat a defenceless animal.' The woman stroked the dog. 'Especially not to abandon a pup. It's downright criminal.'

'It certainly is,' Thea agreed, smiling as the spaniel nudged with its nose at her pocket. 'Oh, you remember, do you? Well, let's have a look at you first, then we'll see if we can find you a biscuit. So, what seems to be the trouble, Mrs Bailey?'

'Well no trouble exactly.' The dark-haired woman frowned. 'We think she's pregnant, although to be honest we don't see quite how it could have happened.' She bit at her lip. 'We're always so careful to make sure the garden gate is kept closed, though one of the tradesmen did leave it open and Cindy got out for a while. Just the once, though.'

'That's all it takes, I'm afraid.' Thea smiled wryly, running a gentle but expert hand over the animal. 'Mm, well, you're right, she's certainly showing all the signs of pregnancy. How long ago would you say it is since she got out?'

'About. . .six weeks.'

'Six weeks.' Thea frowned. 'Well the nipples and breasts are certainly enlarged and her abdomen is distended.'

'She refused her food yesterday and she's suddenly started tearing up papers.'

Thea gave a slight smile. 'Yes, well that's usually a sure sign that a bitch is about to whelp.' She continued her examination, a tiny frown etching its way into her brow. 'In fact——' she straightened up, smiling slightly '—Cindy isn't actually pregnant.'

'But. . .you said she's showing all the signs.' The woman frowned. 'She *looks* pregnant.'

'I know, and that's what makes it so confusing, but what's actually happened is that Cindy is experiencing what we call a false pregnancy,' Thea explained.

'You're right, all the signs are there. Cindy thinks she's pregnant; she has all the symptoms. As far as she's concerned, any day now she should produce a litter of pups.'

The woman's face fell. 'But she isn't going to?'

Thea shook her head. 'I'm afraid not.'

'So what causes this. . .false pregnancy? And can you do anything about it?'

'It's caused by a hormone imbalance,' Thea explained. 'I've checked that there are definitely no puppies. As for what we can do, well, there's no specific treatment as such. You'll probably find that for a couple of weeks or so Cindy will adopt a small toy or a doll, and may generally act a little strangely. But she'll gradually return to normal. In the meantime you should reduce her food intake and make sure she has plenty of exercise to help get rid of the milk. Apart from that, lots of tender, loving care. But I'm sure she gets that anyway.'

It was a normal, busy morning, with the usual varied assortment of conditions requiring treatment. Thea was scrubbing her hands and writing up her notes as Sandra returned with the last patient, a teenager wearing jeans and a thick sweater and carrying a large cardboard box.

'This is Greg.'

'I found this,' he dumped the box unceremoniously on the table, 'over in the woods where they've been chopping down the trees. I thought it might die if I left it on its own, so I brought it in to see if you can do anything with it.'

'This,' as Thea discovered as she carefully opened the box and peered inside, 'was a small owl. She lifted the bird out, restraining it with gentle pressure to prevent it damaging its wings. 'Oh, he's lovely.'

'Yeah, but what is it? I mean, I know it's an owl. . .'

Thea smiled. 'He's a tawny owl. Just a baby from the look of him. He can't have been hatched more than a few days.'

'Isn't he gorgeous?' Sandra moved in closer to take a

look. 'Poor little chap. I wonder what happened to his mum?'

Thea looked at the youth. 'You say someone's been felling trees?'

'Yeah. Me and my mate were up there at the weekend. Some fellas had been up there a couple of days before, getting rid of the storm damage from a month or so back.'

'Yes, I remember it.' Thea frowned. 'I'm afraid that's when we get most of these little chaps brought in. The parents are generally pretty resourceful creatures; they have to be. But having your home come crashing down around your ears is enough to put most animals off.'

'We found him on his own, squeaking his head off and looking pretty sorry for himself. We couldn't just leave him there.'

'No, of course not, although as a general rule if you see a small chick making a lot of noise it's best to leave it alone and see if its parents return. They're usually not far away.' She smiled slightly. 'In this case you did the right thing,' she offered the reassurance.

'So would I be able to keep it, rear it?'

Thea hesitated. 'Would you be able to feed him, four, maybe five times a day?'

Greg frowned. 'It depends. What sort of thing do they eat?'

'Preferably dead day-old chicks.' Thea saw him blanch. 'That would be the ideal. If they aren't available then chopped up raw meat. Not too small, mind. Chicks can swallow pieces much larger than you might imagine. You'd need to add a spot of bonemeal and some sort of roughage, dog or cat hairs, maybe. You may have to open is beak with your fingers at first, to pop the food in, but they soon get the hang of it for themselves.' She looked at Greg. 'The problem is, suppose you manage to rear him — what then?'

He ran a hand through his spiky hair. 'How do you mean?'

'Well, I take it you'd plan on releasing the bird back into the wild.'

He grinned. 'I don't see my mum letting me keep it.'

'No, and in any case it wouldn't be fair to try. So what you have to avoid is imprinting. In other words the bird mustn't get the idea that he's human or belongs with humans. The trick is to touch him as little as possible. In fact,' Thea signalled to Sandra, 'we'll pop this little chap back into his box.'

She settled the chick as Sandra held the box open. 'The less you touch him, the better. Resist the urge to stroke him.' She smiled. 'I know that's not easy but, believe me, you won't be doing the bird any favours, and don't talk to him. It's better that he doesn't become used to the sound of a human voice and begin to think of you as a friend. In the wild he needs to be afraid of humans if he's going to survive.'

Greg was beginning to look distinctly wary. 'It all sounds a bit complicated.'

'It isn't really, although it does need time and patience,' Thea smiled. 'You could keep him in this box to begin with, but eventually you'll need to think about releasing him and you should do that in the evening, but when it's still light, and about four weeks after fledging.'

'And he'd be OK?'

Thea frowned. 'No one can guarantee he'll survive. It's a pretty tough world out there, but if you think you can handle everything. . .'

The youth grinned, raising a hand as he backed towards the door. 'Hey, I don't think so. It's a nice idea but I've got myself a job to go to, starting next week. Anyway, where am I going to get all that raw meat?' He opened the door. 'I'd like to oblige but —— ' he gave a cheeky grin ' — I have to tell you, Doc, he's not my kind of bird.'

Thea gave a rueful smile as she watched him leave, escorted by Sandra. Her head had started to ache and she had to force herself to concentrate on the notes she was writing up, only to find, to her annoyance, that her attention kept wandering.

Without her realising it, a frown darkened her attractive features. From the moment of her arrival three years ago she had fallen in love with the island, with its mingling of French and English, the friendliness of the people. Above all, she had always enjoyed her work, priding herself on her efficiency and the fact that she seemed to have a way with animals, a calming influence almost.

She stabbed the top on and off her pen. If only the same could be said of her own life. It had run perfectly smoothly until now. It was ridiculous the effect Joel Forrester was having on her nerves. She, who had always been so calm, so. . .in charge.

Finishing her notes she pushed the final card away, telling herself decisively that she wouldn't think about Joel Forrester. She was washing her hands when Sandra returned, smiling broadly as she peered into the box where the baby owl raised its head and began squawking again.

'I suppose you're hungry. I'd better see what I can rustle up to tempt you with.' She glanced at Thea. 'It looks like one more for the refuge, then?'

Thea gave a rueful smile. 'It's probably for the best. Wild animals aren't meant to be pets.' She dried her hands, stripping off her white coat and hung it up. 'Where on earth has the morning gone?' She flicked through her diary. 'Were there any messages?'

'Just one. Andrew finished first so he took it. Tom Danby, over at Rosel. It sounds as if one of his pigs has gone down with enteritis. Anyway he said he'll catch up with you later. Oh, I almost forgot, Paul called, about ten minutes ago. You were up to your eyes so I took a message. He said he'll see you later at the Lobster Pot for a quick lunch.'

'Oh, no!' Thea glanced at her watch and stifled a tiny sigh of exasperation. 'Oh, well, bang goes my plan for skipping food and catching up on some of the paperwork.'

'Sorry, did I do the wrong thing?'

'No, it's fine.' Smiling wryly, Thea gathered up a batch of papers, dropping them into her bag. 'I'll just have to go through these tonight. Look, I'd better go. You know where to reach me if you need me. As for you, little fellow — ' she tapped a finger on the box ' — I'll be back for you later.'

'Enjoy your lunch.'

'Will do.' Grabbing a jacket, she hurried out into the now surprisingly chilly air. The tide was on the turn and the small craft were bobbing in the water as she made her way to the harbour and the pub, moving gratefully into its warmth.

It was crowded with locals and early tourists. A fire blazed in the large stone hearth. She spotted Paul as he rose to his feet, waving in her direction.

He kissed her. 'I thought you weren't going to make it.'

'Sorry I'm late.' She smiled in an effort to placate the vague note of censure in his voice. He helped her off with her jacket and she slid into the seat beside him, brushing back her windswept hair. 'It's been a hectic morning.'

'Well, you're here now, that's all that matters. I got you a gin and tonic. Let's eat, shall we?'

She scanned the menu, settling for the lightest thing she could find, a chicken sandwich. The truth was that she rarely stopped for lunch and gin and tonic wasn't something she would have chosen, not with the rest of a busy day still ahead of her. But she sipped at it anyway as Paul headed for the bar, returning seconds later, having refilled his glass.

Their food arrived a surprisingly short time after and they ate surrounded by the busy hubbub of conversation around them.

'Mm, I enjoyed that.' Thea finally sat back, feeling

warm and replete. 'I hadn't realised quite how hungry I was.'

Paul slid an arm round her waist. 'We should do this more often.'

She smiled, relaxed by the atmosphere, letting her hand rest easily in his. 'Chance would be a fine thing. How often do we both manage to be free at the same time? Besides, too many lunches like that and I'd have to do some serious dieting.'

'Nonsense.' He leaned closer to nuzzle her ear and drawled softly. 'There's absolutely nothing wrong with your figure. Take my word for it. I'm a doctor, I should know.'

'I can't help feeling you may be just a shade biased, *Doctor* Prescott.' Her mouth quirked and she stifled a yawn. 'I'm not so sure this was a good idea though. If I sit here much longer I shall fall asleep.'

'I'll try not to wake you.'

'Idiot!' She pushed him gently. 'Some of us still have work to do. Talking of which——' her face became serious '—how are things over at the surgery?'

He moved away, draining his glass and setting it on the table. 'I could do without Mr High and Mighty Forrester looking over my shoulder every time I move. Apart from that——' his lips twisted bitterly '—everything's fine.'

She stared at him unhappily. 'He really is serious, then, about taking over from Bob?'

'Oh, he means it all right. He turned up this morning, as large as life, and took a surgery. He must have been in some time over the weekend and sorted out and removed all the cards for Bob's patients. I can see he's going to be a bastard to work for.'

The vehemence of his words shocked Thea slightly, even while she didn't doubt for a moment that Paul was right. Joel Forrester didn't strike her for a moment as the sort of man who liked seeing his own authority challenged.

'I'm sure Bob must have intended to talk to you

about his future plans for the practice.' She bit at her lower lip. 'Didn't he say anything?'

He shrugged, but she wasn't deceived by the casualness of the gesture. She could tell by his face that he was disturbed by what was happening, and that wasn't like Paul. He was always so easy-going. He toyed with the glass, pushing it along the table.

'You know Bob. He talked about a lot of things — fishing, gardening, walking. Things he planned to do when he retired — but that was always for later.' He raked a hand through his hair. 'I knew he had a nephew. I knew he was something in the medical profession but, to tell you the truth, I didn't take much notice. I mean, he was never around. It didn't seem I was ever likely to meet him.' His fist clenched. 'I can't believe this is happening. After all the work I've put in. . .'

Thea's fingers closed over his hand. 'Look on the bright side,' she urged softly. 'At least now you don't have to cope alone.'

'I think I'd prefer it if I did,' came the disgruntled reply. 'Joel bloody Forrester is already talking about rearranging the entire filing system and extending evening surgery.'

Thea smiled in spite of herself. 'From the little I remember of Bob's filing system, a little reorganisation wouldn't come amiss. As for evening surgery —' her smile faded a little ' — well, I know from experience at the practice that some people find it difficult to get to the surgery until late in the evening. . .'

'Just whose side are you on anyway?' His tone was defensive.

'Oh, Paul, it isn't a question of taking sides. I just think maybe you should give it a chance, that's all,' she reasoned. 'Besides, you know what they say about new brooms sweeping clean. It can't be easy, taking over from Bob. Perhaps he feels he needs to prove something.' Why on earth am I defending the man? she thought. It's not even as if I like him.

Perhaps it was because she allowed her dejection to show briefly in her face that Paul suddenly reached out, drawing her towards him and kissing her on the tip of her nose.

'You're right. I'm being a bore.'

'I didn't say that.'

'You didn't have to.' His finger traced the line of her cheek, then he glanced up at the clock and frowned. 'Damn! It's time I wasn't here. I hate to break things up but I've got to make a move.'

Thea was already hunting frantically for her bag. 'Heavens, is that the time? She waited while Paul settled the bill and minutes later they emerged into the fresh air and a near-empty car park.

She stood docilely in the circle of Paul's arms, her face turned up to his, and experienced a tiny *frisson* of shock as another face imposed itself in her thoughts. Darker, more rugged and altogether too disturbing for comfort. 'Thank you for a lovely lunch,' she said breathlessly. 'I enjoyed it.'

'So did I. I'll ring you tonight.' Paul's lips brushed hers. It was a nice kiss, undemanding, nothing earth-shattering. Safe, the way she liked it.

'I hate to intrude,' the deep voice came from behind them, and Thea broke away, spinning round to find herself staring into an all too familiar face.

Joel Forrester stood beside his own car. It wasn't only the aggressive stance which took her breath away, it was the raised eyebrows, the derisive smile playing around his lips as he said tersely, 'I called at the surgery. They told me I'd probably find you here.' His glance swept over Paul before coming to rest on herself, leaving Thea only too conscious of her dishevelled appearance.

'You went to the surgery. . .?' She broke off, her face suddenly wearing an expression of dismay. 'It's not Wellie? He's not worse?'

'Wellie's fine.' Joel's gaze shifted, his expression

darkening briefly. 'Correct me if I'm wrong, but don't you have a clinic this afternoon, Prescott?'

Paul gathered his car keys and looked at Thea. 'Yes, well, I'd better be on my way. I'll talk to you later.' With a tight-lipped glance in her direction, he sped away.

Thea was scarcely aware of him leaving, heading for his own car as her gaze returned to the man standing before her. She felt her breath catch in her throat. Wearing jeans he had been impressive. Dressed in the dark suit, the material stretched taut against the hard muscles of his thighs, he looked powerfully masculine.

She dragged her gaze away. 'Yes, well, I'm sorry, Doctor, but I really don't have time to stand and chat.' It was disconcerting to find her hand shaking as she shrugged herself into her jacket. She fumbled clumsily, trying to disentangle the sleeve. It remained stubbornly stuck.

Joel's arm came around her, the contact sending a kind of electric shock running through her. 'Here, let me help.' He was so close that she could see the firm texture of his skin, smell the subtle tang of an expensive aftershave. She felt a tremor of something closely akin to excitement run through her. No matter how much she might dislike Joel Forrester's arrogance, there was no denying that he possessed an animal magnetism. She straightened up, alarmed by the direction her thoughts had suddenly taken.

'Thea, wait.' He gave her a quick glance, a half-smile tugging at his lips. 'I don't bite, you know. I need your help, that's all. I have to visit a patient and I'd be grateful if you'd go with me.'

CHAPTER FIVE

'Go with. . .?' Thea stared at him incredulously and gave a slight laugh. 'In case you've forgotten, I'm a vet, not a doctor. The difference may be subtle but I think your patients might just notice.'

He smiled drily. 'I have to go out to Grouville, to see old Mrs Pemberton. A neighbour called the surgery to say she's had a fall.'

'Maggie has? Oh, no! Is she hurt?'

His dark brows drew together. 'You know her?'

'Yes.' Thea frowned. 'Not very well. I don't think anyone does. She's slightly eccentric, getting on a bit, lives alone.' Her troubled gaze levelled with his. 'How serious is it?'

'It's hard to say. It sounds pretty bad. I'm probably going to have to get her admitted to hospital. That's why I need your help.'

'I still don't see how. . .'

His mouth tightened. 'If you know her you'll know the set-up at that place. I haven't been out there for years, not since I was a kid. Bob occasionally used to take me with him on his rounds.' Joel raked a hand through his hair. 'You said yourself, Maggie's an eccentric. I doubt whether things have changed. There were always a dozen or more stray cats wandering around, not to mention the odd dog.'

Thea gave a wry smile. 'You're forgetting the donkey.'

'Donkey?' A glint of humour briefly lit his dark eyes.

Thea nodded. 'She acquired it—rescued it. I don't think anyone's quite sure. But she keeps it in one of the fields along with the goat.'

'Well obviously they can't be left to fend for themselves.' He frowned. 'As I see it we have two choices;

62

either the animals have to be moved and cared for, or put down.'

Thea studied him unhappily. 'You're not serious?'

A spasm flickered across his face. 'Do you have a better suggestion? My responsibility is to my patient. I know Maggie Pemberton well enough to know she won't allow herself to be taken away from that place if it means leaving her animals. Someone has to persuade her.' His dark brows drew together. 'You can persuade her. She knows you, she trusts you.'

Thea drew a long, shaky breath then nodded. 'All right. I'll come.'

'Good girl. We'll take my car.'

'Have you given any thought as to what, precisely, we're going to do with this. . .this miniature menagerie?' she said as she climbed into the passenger seat beside him.

Joel gazed at the road ahead, grinning. 'I was rather hoping you were going to come up with an answer to that one.'

She shot him a look, sank back into the seat, sighing with exasperation, and was still pondering the problem as they drew up at the small farm holding ten minutes later.

The door opened before they could reach it. 'She's through here.' An anxious-looking woman of about forty led them through a dimly lit hallway into the sitting-room where Maggie Pemberton lay on the floor in front of an ancient sofa. Her eyes were closed, her weather-lined face drawn with pain.

At seventy-five, Maggie had worked hard all her life, making few concessions to the cold of winter or her own advancing years. Even now, with a fire burning in the old black lead grate, the small cottage could hardly be described as cosy.

'I called round to buy a few eggs and found her lying on the floor. I'm Val Redmond, by the way. I called you.' She bit her lip anxiously. 'I didn't move her. I didn't know what to do so I covered her with a blanket. . .'

Joel smiled reassuringly. 'You did exactly the right thing.' In one calm, unhurried movement he was kneeling beside the elderly woman to make a gentle examination.

'Maggie, can you hear me? It's Joel, Joel Forrester,' he said gently. 'I gather you've had a bit of a fall. No, don't try to move.' He stroked her hand, smiling, as her eyelids fluttered open. 'You're going to be fine. I just need to find out what the damage is.'

She gave a soft groan of pain. 'My leg,' she said weakly, 'and my chest.' One frail hand fluttered in the direction of her ribs. 'I came over a bit dizzy. Next thing I knew, I was on the floor. I tried to get up but it hurt too much.'

Joel's expression betrayed nothing as he made his examination, the strong hands moving with surprising gentleness until he relaxed and straightened up.

'I think you may have a cracked rib, Maggie. We're going to need an X-ray to find out for sure. You're going to have a few nasty bruises on that leg too for a while, but, apart from that, you're lucky, I'm pretty sure it's not broken. I'm afraid it does mean hospital for a while, though.'

Maggie's eyes filled with tears. 'But I can't leave the farm. Who'll look after my animals? They need me.'

'Perhaps I could pack a few things in a bag?'

'We'll work something out, Maggie,' Joel said gently, nodding in Val Redmond's direction. 'It won't be for long. Besides,' he flicked a smiling glance in Thea's direction, 'that's why I brought Miss Somers along. You know Thea? Yes, of course you do. Well she's our resident animal expert and she's going to take care of things. Now I'm just going to give you a small injection, a pain-killer, to ease things while we move you, and to keep you going until we see what the real damage is.'

He shot a look in Thea's direction, nodding almost imperceptibly towards the door.

'I'll make some tea,' Thea swallowed hard and headed for the kitchen.

'I think it might be a good idea if you were to ring for an ambulance as well,' Joel said quietly as he straightened up, moving with her towards the door on the pretext of getting his bag.

'You're worried about her, aren't you?' Thea murmured. 'I mean more than you're letting her know.'

His dark brows drew together. 'She's frail and we don't know for sure just how long she's been lying there. Apart from that you only have to look at her to see she hasn't been eating properly for some time. I suspect she's got a bit of a chest infection bubbling away in there too.' He glanced briefly round the tiny, old-fashioned kitchen. 'In a way it may turn out to be a blessing in disguise that this has happened now. I'm not saying it's good that she was injured, but if we hadn't been given a reason to come out here I wouldn't have given much for her chances of getting through another winter. . .' He broke off. 'Look, forget the tea. It might be a good idea if you take a quick look around and see what we're up against.'

She nodded. 'I'll ring for the ambulance on my way.'

'Thea?' She half-turned in the doorway almost colliding with his taut muscular frame. He stared down at her and her pulse-rate accelerated dangerously. Her lips parted on a little gasp as his mouth brushed against hers. 'I just wanted to say thanks.'

Watching the door close behind him, she was conscious of the warm colour surging into her cheeks. Careful, she told herself firmly, as she hurried breathlessly out into the yard, glad of the chill wind that took the colour from her cheeks. Remember, he's not your type, and anyway, what was one kiss? He was grateful, that's all, just grateful, so don't go reading anything into it.

Returning minutes later, after a quick reconnaissance of the small holding, she found Joel sitting on the sofa, holding Maggie's hand. She was pleased to see the older woman smiling, though there was still a note of anxiety in her voice.

'I don't have to go, do I? I don't want to go.'

'It would be best, Maggie,' Joel advised gently. 'In any case, if, as I suspect, that rib is cracked, how would you manage? You wouldn't be able to get around too easily, and the animals would still need feeding.'

'But I've never been away before, not even when George was alive.' Maggie's blue-veined hand fondled the large cat draped across her knee; another watched from a chair. Tears welled up again. 'I don't want to go. I'll manage. . .'

'You mustn't worry about the animals, Maggie,' Thea moved to sit beside her. 'If you like, I can take the cats over to the refuge, just until you feel well enough to cope again. I promise,' she said, 'I'll look after them all as if they were my own, and I'm sure Mrs Redmond will feed the chickens for you.'

'Yes, of course I will,' the other woman smiled. 'And I'm sure our Jack would take care of the goat as well. He's always been fascinated by it. I have to keep telling him not to come pestering. . .'

'He's a good boy. Oh, dear,' Maggie glanced anxiously towards the window at the sound of a vehicle pulling up in the yard.

'That will be the ambulance.' Joel was on his feet. 'You'll be fine, Maggie. Everything will still be here when you come back, exactly as you left it. All you have to do is get better, and I'm going to do everything I can to make sure it happens.'

He means it, Thea thought, and, more to the point, Maggie believes it. Patients, whether of the human or the animal variety, weren't easily fooled. They knew, instinctively, when they were being lied or condescended to.

It was another hour before they arrived back at the refuge. They were unloading the hastily contrived boxes with their indignant occupants into cages when, totally illogically, reaction set in and, for a brief moment, as tears welled up, Thea closed her eyes, only to open them again quickly as Joel's hand tightened on her arm.

'Are you all right?'

'What?' Thea blinked hard, 'Oh, yes, I'm fine.'

His gaze narrowed. 'I want to thank you again for what you did, for the way you handled Maggie, and for taking this lot on.'

'I didn't do a thing.' She sighed, suddenly very weary. 'In fact, if I'm honest, I felt completely useless.' She shook her head. 'I don't think I could do your job.'

His dark brows rose mockingly. 'You mean the animals can't fight back?'

Her head rose indignantly, and she blushed as the memory of those few seconds she had spent in his arms came surging back so vividly that she jerked away in an effort not to let him see the effect it had on her.

'Thea, what's wrong?' His grasp tightened, turning her to face him when she would have moved away. His touch sent a shuddering heat through her veins. She drew a deep breath, her face taut with strain.

'I've known Maggie for almost three years, ever since I came to the island.' She brushed a hand through her hair. 'I've been out to treat various animals at one time or another, but I had no idea. . .' Her voice broke. 'Being in that cottage was like being caught in some kind of time warp.' She gave a short laugh. 'I doubt if Maggie even knows what a microwave is. She probably wouldn't use a washing machine even if she had one. It's as if. . .as if nothing in the house has changed for a hundred years, and she copes, struggles. . .'

Joel's face darkened. 'You're probably right. In a way nothing has changed, at least not for the past twenty years.' He saw the tiny frown furrow her brow. 'Not since George died. Before that, Maggie was a regular churchgoer; she took part in most local events. After. . .' He shook his head. 'It was as if she lost interest, decided to shut herself away.'

'But that's terrible.' Her grey-green eyes clouded. 'Didn't anyone know, or care, how she was living.'

Joel frowned. 'That's not what I'm saying. It was Maggie's choice.'

She stared at him and gave a slight laugh of derision. 'But surely someone is responsible?'

'Oh, we're all responsible, but you must know that Maggie didn't exactly welcome visitors, and she's entitled to her privacy.'

'Privacy!' She stiffened, trying to pull away. 'She could have lain there for days. She could have died and no one would have been any the wiser if it weren't for the fact that Mrs Redmond decided she needed to buy some eggs. I'd say that comes pretty close to neglect.'

His mouth hardened. 'It isn't an ideal world out there, Thea.'

Her eyes widened in disbelief. 'You're damn right it isn't. So are you saying that someone like Maggie, any old person, can simply close their front door and it's all right to forget about them. Out of sight, out of mind, is that it?'

'No, that isn't what I'm saying.' His hands tightened on her arms. 'But people have a right to choose what they want, how they want to live. You and I both know that, ideally, someone like Maggie would be better off in some sort of unit where all her physical needs would be provided. But what about the rest? What sort of life do you think she would have, closed in, without her animals, without the fields?' he said roughly. 'I'm just a doctor. That doesn't give me the right to play God.'

For a moment she stared at him in stunned silence. 'So, you'll patch her up and send her home, knowing full well it could happen all over again, except that, next time, it might be worse.' Her voice held an edge of scorn. 'Or maybe that would be more convenient. It would certainly save everyone a lot of trouble, wouldn't it, Doctor?'

She knew she had gone too far when his eyes narrowed to glittering slits. His grasp tightened, drawing her closer. 'You're getting the whole thing out of proportion,' he ground out. 'Maybe you're right to stick to treating animals. They don't make demands, they don't require emotional involvement.' His mouth twisted. 'If they did you probably wouldn't be able to handle it, would you, Thea? Or would you? Maybe it's time we found out.'

'Why, you. . .' Her face flamed as he drew her roughly towards him. It wasn't true, she wanted to shout. Treating animals wasn't some sort of easy option, it didn't provide some sort of safety cut-out for her own emotions.

But she wasn't given the chance. She began to struggle as he bent his head towards her. She told herself she would feel nothing as he moulded her into the muscular hardness of his thighs. She tried to pull away, but found she couldn't.

As if in slow motion his mouth brushed hers in a kiss that was so unexpectedly sensuous that she was mesmerised by it. The slow thud of her own heartbeat sounded dully in her ears. Her senses reeled and, to her everlasting shame, a totally new sensation coursed through her, so unlike anything she had ever experienced before that she gasped as her body betrayed her with its own response.

In all the times Paul had kissed her it had never been like this. Joel Forrester was the most sexually exciting man she had ever met. An involuntary shiver ran through her and she stared up at him blindly for a few seconds, aware of an unaccountable feeling of loss when finally he drew away.

'I think maybe it's time I took you home,' he breathed, 'before I do something we might both regret.'

He released her so quickly that she wondered afterwards whether he had actually said the words or she had imagined them.

Back at the cottage she closed the door firmly behind her and wandered into the sitting-room to sit staring at the blank television screen, trying to work out what it all meant.

It was ridiculous to allow one simple kiss to affect her in such a way. A kiss which, after all, certainly couldn't have meant anything to a man like Joel Forrester, who had made it quite clear precisely what he thought of her. All the same, her hand shook as she raked it through her hair, acknowledging, grudgingly, that for a few seconds at least the brief contact had had a most extraordinary effect upon her emotions.

Sighing heavily, she rose to her feet and walked briskly into the kitchen, wondering for one tantalising moment what it would be like to be kissed properly by him, and then she dismissed it, slamming the fridge door heavily to a close on the thought that such speculation was not only highly dangerous, it was totally irrelevant.

CHAPTER SIX

'STILL busy?'

'Andrew.' Thea looked up from the neat row of stitching she had just completed and rubbed at the ache in her back. 'No, come in. This is the last. Would you like to take him, Sandra?' She handed the sleeping puppy over to her assistant. 'Just keep an eye on him. I'll check him over later, then, all being well, his owner can collect him tomorrow morning.'

'Will do.' Smiling, Sandra carried the small bundle away and Thea turned her attention to the senior partner.

'So what's this, then?' She grinned. 'Extended coffee break?'

'Ssh! I'm praying the phone won't ring.' Andrew spoke from the doorway. He was carrying his jacket slung over one shoulder and sauntered in to toss it on to a chair. 'I promised Joanne we'd go into town to take a look at some new curtain material she's been hankering after and apparently I also rashly mentioned something about lunch.'

'Very nice, too. Some people have all the luck.'

'Come with us. You know you're more than welcome.' He eyed the Thermos on a tray. 'Is that fresh coffee?' He lifted the lid, inhaling deeply. 'Ah, a lifesaver. Joanne is always complaining she doesn't get to see enough of you and she's got more time on her hands, now that the boys are back at school.'

'Oh, I'd love to, honestly.' Thea took the cup he offered, stirring in sugar. 'But I can't, not today anyway,' she said with genuine regret. 'I promised to meet Paul. He's at the magistrates' court. Something to do with a childcare case.'

'Mm, they can get a bit depressing.'

'Yes, I know. That's why I thought it might be a good idea to have a change of scene.' She frowned. 'We don't seem to get too much time together these days. For some reason we always seem to be heading in opposite directions.' A tiny feeling of depression hovered like a small black cloud as she shed her white coat, checking her appearance in the small mirror. 'The trouble is, some of these cases can drag on. Still, it's worth a try, even if we only manage to grab a quick sandwich afterwards.'

Andrew nodded sympathetically. 'It can't have been easy since Bob died, but I imagine things should get slightly less hectic, now that Joel's back and taking over at the surgery.' He frowned. 'It's a damn shame the old man wasn't round long enough to see it happen. It's what he always wanted, you know — the pair of them, working together. By the way ——' he delved, grinning, into a biscuit tin '— I didn't realise you were planning a change in direction careerwise, as they say.' Thea stared at him and he laughed. 'I heard you were with Joel, up at Maggie Pemberton's place.'

'Oh, yes.' She bit at her lower lip. 'Look, I'm really sorry about landing the practice with those kittens. I took as many of the older cats as I could but those two didn't look as if they were going to make it.'

'Hey ——' Grinning, he raised a hand. 'I'm not complaining. You were right, they were pretty badly undernourished. God knows what Maggie feeds them on.'

'They probably just have to take their chances in the fields.'

'You could be right at that. Anyway, I've started them off on a diet supplement. With a bit of luck they should be fine. So, what's happening to Maggie?'

'At the moment she's in hospital.' Thea sipped gratefully at her coffee. 'Joel was obviously worried about her. The trouble is, I suspect she won't make an easy patient. She didn't want to go. I think it was mainly down to Joel's powers of persuasion and knowing that her animals would be looked after that tipped the balance.'

'Mm, but surely you can't manage them all?'

Thea gave a slight smile. It was a thought that had helped to keep her awake for much of the night. How was she going to manage? Her meagre resources were already stretched and, as it was, she found herself relying more and more on voluntary contributions to keep the refuge going. But there was a limit to how much she could expect from other people. She sighed. No, somehow or other she would simply have to manage, even if it meant tightening her own belt a little.

Forcing a smile, she said airily, 'It'll be a bit of a squeeze but I can take most of them, for a while anyway. Hopefully it won't be for too long. Luckily, Maggie's neighbour offered to keep an eye on the goat and the donkey. Oh, and——' she looked at him uncertainly '—I said if she was at all worried to give us a call here at the practice. I'll cover it, of course. . .'

'Rubbish. Maggie's been a client for more years than I care to remember. The least we can do is see her through a rough patch.'

Thea smiled. 'You're a softie, you know that?'

He gave an answering grin. 'Just don't let the word get around, that's all.' He glanced at his watch. 'Help! I shouldn't be here.' His cup and saucer rattled on to the tray. 'Catch you later.'

'Bye.' Thea smiled wryly at the departing figure.

An hour later, casting an anxious look at the overcast sky, she parked her Land Rover in the car park adjoining the large shopping centre, locked it and, with twenty minutes to spare before she had to meet Paul, decided to investigate the main shopping area.

She couldn't remember the last time she had just browsed. The new window display in one of the many boutiques caught her eye and on impulse she wandered in to find herself confronted by rails filled with the spring season's newest fashions.

'Is madam looking for anything in particular?' A sales assistant glided towards her.

'What? Oh, no, not really.' Thea smiled. 'I didn't actually intend coming in, but I must admit the colours in the new display caught my eye.'

'Our latest line in partywear. Yes, we're rather pleased with it,' the girl enthused, 'and if you don't mind my saying so, the new season's colours would look just perfect with madam's colouring.' She swept one of the garments from the rail. 'Why don't you just slip it on, see how you like it?'

How did I let myself get talked into this? Thea stood in the cubicle, resignedly stripping to her undies and stepping into the dress.

I've a perfectly good dress at home, she told herself firmly. So suitable that you've trotted it out so many times, people will begin to get the idea it's the only thing in your wardrobe, some inner voice took an unfair swipe at her conscience. And what about Andrew and Joanne's party?

She peered at the price tag and winced. But when she looked at her reflection in the mirror, studying the line of the figure-hugging burgundy dress, she knew she was fighting a losing battle. It did look good, she had to admit. With her hair curling loosely against her shoulders, her cheeks still flushed from the chilly wind, it seemed somehow to emphasise the green of her eyes.

'I'll take it.' And bang goes this week's housekeeping, she thought, sighing heavily.

By the time she came out of the shop carrying the large carrier bag, it was past midday and her stomach was rumbling. Sprinting across the road, she headed for a well-known coffee shop and was relieved to find Paul already waiting for her at one of the tables.

He rose to his feet to greet her and she found herself thinking, not for the first time, that he had the sort of fair-haired good looks that would always turn heads. Not the dark, dramatic sort of looks, maybe. Even so, there was something nice about being the recipient of that smile.

She sat down, smiling breathlessly. 'I wasn't sure you'd make it.' Having given her order to the waiter she sat back. 'So, how did the hearing go?'

He shrugged. 'Pretty much as expected. I said my bit, everyone else did the same. In the end the magistrates agreed and made a care order.'

'Oh, well, that's good, isn't it?'

He frowned. 'At least it means the child in question probably won't get beaten, for a while anyway. So —' he sat back as their sandwiches and coffee arrived '— I feel my feeble efforts on this occasion at least have not entirely been in vain.'

'Oh, dear.' Thea deliberately injected a note of lightness into her voice. 'That bad?'

He had the grace to smile. 'It's nothing. Put it down to a bad couple of days, that's all.'

Thea pushed her chicken sandwich round the plate and finally abandoned it altogether. 'I missed you yesterday.'

'I missed you too.' He grinned. 'We'll have to stop meeting like this. People will start to talk.' He squeezed her hand. 'Look, it's impossible to make yourself heard in here. Shall we get out?'

He was right. Within the space of half an hour the café had begun to fill as people crowded in to make the most of their lunch breaks.

Slipping out of her seat, Thea followed him to the door. It was almost a relief to walk into the brightening afternoon, on to pavements dampened by a recent shower of rain.

Paul looked at his watch. 'I should be getting back. There's a baby clinic this afternoon. How about you?'

She shook her head. 'Now that I'm here I thought I might do a bit of shopping, but I'll walk with you, then at least we can talk.'

He turned, pulling her towards him, and, with an eagerness which took her slightly by surprise, slipped an arm round her waist and kissed her soundly. Releasing her, he gave a sheepish grin. 'That's just to say I'm sorry. I know I'm not very good company just lately. I don't mean to be a grouch.'

'Don't be silly,' she said softly. 'I understand.' Tucking a stray strand of hair back into place, she smiled. 'If this is what being taken out to lunch does, perhaps we should do it more often.' And then, more seriously, 'I know things haven't been easy, but they're bound to sort themselves out, sooner or later. It's early days yet.'

'I hope you're right,' he said testily. 'Because, to be honest, I don't think I can take much more, the way things are. At least with Bob I thought I knew where I stood. This chap Forrester seems to spend the entire time trying to put me in my place and finding fault.'

Thea bit her lip, sighing inwardly at the prospect, yet again, of being caught in a battle between two seemingly immovable objects. She couldn't quite keep the note of exasperation out of her voice as she said, 'What happened?'

'Oh, it was crazy, ridiculous. I've gone along with him on the change of surgery hours. God knows,' he raked a hand through his hair, 'I didn't have much choice. I've even agreed to an appointments system, rather than patients just turning up at the surgery.'

There was a note in his voice which Thea tried to ignore as she frowned, thoughtfully. She could see that, for patients who had to travel some distance to the surgery, an appointments system might have its advantages, but, knowing Joel Forrester, he had probably made the decision in his usual, arrogant manner, without consultation. 'Oh, Paul,' she murmured softly.

'But the final straw came when he actually had the nerve to criticise my treatment of a patient. He had the gall to accuse me of negligence.'

Thea bit her lip. 'Oh, I find that hard to believe.' She put her hand on his arm. 'You must have misunderstood, or perhaps he didn't understand the particular situation.'

He shook her hand off. 'Oh, he understood all right,' he said testily. 'Some old dear had an accident a couple of months back. It wasn't the first time. It's not as if it was anything too serious, a sprained ankle or something. I can't remember exactly.' The colour rose in his neck as he was speaking. 'If you ask me, she'd have been better off in a home where she could be properly supervised, and I said so at the time. Anyway, I gather it's happened again. They've carted the old lady off to hospital and Forrester actually had the nerve to play hell because I hadn't done a follow-up visit, and, to add insult to injury, he's talking about getting a replacement.'

'I'm sure he wouldn't.' Thea bit at her lower lip. 'This patient. . . I'm not asking you to break any confidences, of course, but, it wouldn't by any chance be Maggie Pemberton?'

'Yes, as a matter of fact, it was.' He frowned peevishly. 'The damnable part of it is, I had intended seeing her again, but you know how it is? There just never seems to be enough time.'

Thea nodded, saying nothing, but she couldn't help thinking that maybe that one visit would have made all the difference to Maggie. Still, she could imagine the sort of tension Paul must be up against and she smiled sympathetically.

'I'm sure it will all sort itself out.'

'I hope you're right, because I'm getting pretty fed up of being made the whipping boy.' He drew her towards him again, kissing her cheek. 'You're good for my morale, you know that?' He nuzzled her ear. 'God, I needed to talk to you. . .'

'Talking of which,' she smiled, 'I could have done with a chat myself. I called you last night, but you were out.'

She wondered if she had imagined the slightly sheepish look which flickered across his good-looking features, then knew she hadn't as he said reluctantly, 'Ah, yes, last night. I suppose I'd better come clean before the local bush telegraph gets to work. As a matter of fact I was feeling a bit fed up so I went out for a drink with Linda Sawson. You know Linda?'

'Isn't she the surgery receptionist?'

'That's right. Well, apparently she applied for a new job and wanted to talk, so it seemed like a good idea and I knew you wouldn't mind. Honestly, we both needed to unwind.' He laughed slightly. 'It was all quite innocent, a bit of a bore to be perfectly honest. You know how it is?'

'Yes, I'm sure it was,' Thea murmured, wondering with a slight tremor of shock why he should be so defensive if what he said was true.

It was disconcerting to discover that there was a tiny chink in the veil of security she had built around herself. 'Of course I believe you. Anyway,' she forced a note of brightness into her voice, 'you're a free agent. It's not as if we're engaged. You're perfectly entitled to go out with whom you like.'

She saw the faint colour steal into his face. 'You're not jealous?'

'No, of course not,' she said briskly. But was that entirely true? she wondered as she made her way thoughtfully back to the shopping centre. She needed time to analyse her feelings. It had come as a shock to realise that Paul had actually taken someone else out, but it was her he had kissed. . .

'Look out!'

Deep in thought, head down, she wasn't even aware of her surroundings until a hand came down sharply on her arm, jerking her out of the path of the car into which she had almost stepped.

'God, I might have known it would be you. I have a full quota of patients already, without having to resort to people who throw themselves under cars.'

Desperately trying to regain her balance, she clutched at the nearest available object and felt the colour surge into her cheeks as she stared, breathlessly, up into the face of Joel Forrester.

She groaned inwardly. Oh, no! Of all people, why did it have to be him?

'Still causing havoc, Thea? Are you all right?' Concern sounded in his voice.

'Yes, thank you. I. . . I'm fine.' She brushed at her coat. 'I'm sorry, I don't know what I was thinking about.' She struggled to free herself, an unfamiliar tightness gripping her stomach as slowly she became aware of the girl who stood beside Joel, watching with amused interest.

'I'm glad I'm not the only one. Still, if you're going to get knocked down, best have a doctor around, I always say.'

She was attractive, with the kind of looks and diminutive height that probably had men queuing up to rescue her. Around thirty, with pansy-brown eyes, chicly styled black hair and a heart-shaped face you wouldn't mind seeing in the mirror in the mornings, Thea thought uncharitably.

'I don't know if you know Helen? Thea, Helen Crawford. Helen, Thea Somers.'

'Yes, of course. You work with Andrew Tyler at the local veterinary practice, don't you? I've seen you around.'

'Mrs Crawford.' Thea's smile was fixed as she offered her hand to the other woman.

'It's Miss, actually, and please, call me Helen. Joel and I have just been to a meeting.' She pulled a face. 'I was beginning to think it would go on for ever.'

Thea was acutely conscious of her own slightly windswept appearance beside the professional perfection of the other woman in her dark blue uniform dress and coat. Unruly tendrils seemed to have escaped from her own French plait, drifting against her neck in wispy curls, and she was aware of the deepening flush spreading across her cheeks as she studiously avoided Joel's gaze.

'Helen is our senior district nurse, apart from being a leading light in the local community.'

Helen laughed, displaying perfectly even, white teeth. 'Don't take any notice. He exaggerates, but then, he always did.'

'You. . .know each other well, then?' Thea's throat felt suddenly dry and she was confused by a sudden welter of emotions she absolutely refused to acknowledge.

Joel's mouth curved. 'Oh, Helen and I go back a long way. There was even a time when I thought I might persuade her to become a doctor.'

'I'm quite happy doing what I do, thank you very much. We also serve and all that. Talking of which——' she turned her smiling gaze on Thea '—I've been trying to persuade Joel to take a more active part in the community, now that he's back. I have to admit, there's also a mercenary motive. We have an emergency. It's the local spring fête in a few weeks' time and one of our committee members has had to drop out. You know Councillor Drew? Well his wife died recently and, understandably, he feels unable to cope with the extra work involved in organising things. So, we're looking for someone to replace him and judge the cakes and jams and I'm trying to talk Joel into it but he's being stubborn, as usual.'

Thea flicked a glance in the direction of the cool, blue gaze and wished she hadn't as her eyes encountered his mouth, firm and attractive and far too much of a threat to her peace of mind right now.

With a supreme effort she hauled back her wayward thoughts. 'I'm sure you couldn't find anyone better qualified,' she said evenly, 'and it is, after all, in a good cause.'

His mouth quirked. 'In that case, I'll make a bargain with you. I'm prepared to do my bit if you're prepared to do yours.'

She moistened her lips with the tip of her tongue. 'I don't know what you mean.'

'It's quite simple. I'll judge the jams and cakes if you're prepared to take on the babies.'

'B-but that's not fair,' she spluttered.

Blue eyes glinted. 'As you say, it's all in a good cause, Miss Somers. We'd be delighted to do our bit.'

'Oh, that's marvellous.' Helen Crawford beamed.

Thea threw him a malevolent look.

'I can't tell you how relieved I am and I know the fête committee will be enormously grateful. Oh, heavens, is that the time? Joel, I must fly. I've still got a couple of calls to make.'

'I'll catch up with you later.' He dropped a kiss lightly on her cheek, waving as she disappeared towards the car park.

And I'll bet he doesn't have to run too hard, Thea thought ungraciously.

'Well, so where to now, then?'

A slow tide of angry colour rose in her cheeks as she rounded on him. 'How *dare* you do that to me?' She swayed slightly on unaccustomed high heels.

'Do what?' His face assumed an innocent expression which didn't fool her for one minute.

'You know very well what.' Furiously, Thea shrugged away his supporting arm as she forced her foot back into her shoe. A three-inch heel gave her an advantage over a lot of men but not this one. 'You had no right to . . .to force me into a commitment. Besides——' she squared her shoulders, purposely ignoring the sardonic gleam in his eyes '—I don't know the first thing about babies,' she added defiantly.

'Why, Thea Somers, shame on you.' He raised a mocking eyebrow. 'As a matter of fact, I don't know the first thing about cakes and jam except that they come off a supermarket shelf. . .'

'Heathen,' she muttered. 'Just let the ladies of the WI get to hear.'

'It seems we both have a lot to learn,' he said softly. 'But at least it's all in a good cause, so it looks as if we're just going to have to grin and bear it.'

'You could have said no.'

His mouth quirked. 'You obviously don't know

Helen. She's a very determined lady. Once her mind is set on something, she usually gets it.'

Including Joel Forrester? Thea felt her skin pale. Weariness suddenly washed over her. She looked at her watch. 'I have to go. Duty calls. If you'll excuse me.'

'Thea, wait.' His hand rested lightly on her arm. 'I haven't thanked you properly for what you did the other day, over at Maggie Pemberton's place. I couldn't have managed without you.'

She turned, with an effort keeping her voice even. 'How is she?'

'A lot happier, knowing that her animals are being cared for. I think she sees them as some sort of lifeline.'

'Most elderly people become very attached to their pets. They pine for them if they have to go into hospital. It can work both ways. Animals miss their owners too.'

Joel frowned. 'I've heard of some sort of scheme, where people can have their pets visit them in hospital.'

'Oh, you mean Pat-a-Dog.'

'Pat-a-Dog?'

'That's right.' Thea smiled, relaxing as she felt herself on safer ground. 'It's becoming very popular. What happens is that pet owners, volunteers from the community, go along to hospitals, elderly care establishments, maybe even someone's home, taking along a dog and spending some time chatting to the person who, literally, strokes the animal, talks to it. Obviously we have to be one hundred per cent sure the animal is docile and friendly.'

'Obviously.'

She shot him a look. 'I suppose you think the idea is too quaint for words?'

'Quite the contrary,' he said evenly. 'In fact there's strong medical evidence to back up the theory that stroking an animal can have a calming effect and dramatically reduce high blood pressure. I say if a system works, go with it.'

'Y-you do?'

There was silence for a moment. 'Have you tried the scheme locally?'

'Well, no.'

'Why not?'

She stared at him. 'Well, I suppose no one has actually got around to organising it. Are you saying you approve?'

'Absolutely. My job is to make people better. That's likely to be easier if they aren't fretting for their pets. I think it might be worth while giving this idea some serious consideration. What do you say?'

She smiled. 'I'd love to. So what do you suggest?'

'I'll need to sound out a few people.' They started to walk together, his hand coming round her waist as she side-stepped to avoid the bustle of shoppers. 'Perhaps we could start by taking Wellie to one of the local rest homes, as soon as he's well enough, of course. Most people around here know him. We could go together. What do you think?'

When he looked at her like that, with those startlingly blue eyes, she wasn't even sure she knew what she was thinking.

Flustered, she nodded. 'If you can arrange it, I'm all for it.'

'Good. I'll let you know.'

They crossed the road, heading for the car park. She would have to do her shopping another day, Thea thought. She said, 'You really do love your work, don't you?'

He frowned. 'It has its rewarding moments. There's a down-side too, of course. But yes, it's good. I get a lot of job satisfaction. But that's something you must know all about.'

Reaching the Land Rover, she fumbled for her keys, cursing softly as they fell to the floor.

'Here, let me.' In one fluid movement he swept them up, placing them in her hands.

She felt the breath catch in her throat as a feeling of

physical awareness swept through her, then she pulled her hand out of his grasp. 'Thank you.'

'Think nothing of it. Here, perhaps you'd better let me.' Taking them from her, he bent his head to unlock the door and she found herself gazing with fascination at his hair which curled slightly against his collar.

A small pulse hammered in her throat. 'You. . .you must find things very different here, after Canada. Doesn't it bother you, coming back to a small rural practice after all that open space?'

He laughed. 'Canada isn't all wide open spaces. Anyway, it was always planned,' he said, evenly. 'I expected to take over the practice when my uncle retired. It was what we both wanted.' He frowned. 'Sadly, it didn't work out that way.'

'You don't have any regrets?'

'About not being here when he died? Yes, of course I regret that. But I don't feel that my years in Canada or my time with VSO were wasted. They helped to broaden my experience as nothing else could.'

'Won't you find it difficult to settle?'

His shoulders moved dismissively. 'I'd completed my contract anyway.'

'How long before you feel the need to move on again?' she ventured.

His mouth quirked. 'Trying to get rid of me, Thea?'

Her colour rose. 'Don't give me ideas.' But he hadn't answered the question, she noted. Joel Forrester, here today, gone tomorrow.

His blue eyes narrowed as he gave her a sidelong glance. 'Tell me about you and Prescott.'

'Paul?' Colour flared into her cheeks. 'Why?'

'Idle curiosity.'

'There's nothing to tell. We became friends shortly after Paul arrived to help out at the practice.' She turned slowly to find him watching her, an unreadable expression in his blue eyes. 'Paul is a good doctor. He does care. I don't think you've been entirely fair. . .'

'I admire your loyalty —— ' for a second there was a

flash of cynicism in his eyes '—even if he doesn't deserve it.'

'That's not true. You haven't given him a chance.'

'He's no good for you, you know?' Joel drawled softly.

'And I suppose you know what is?' She felt an odd, fluttering sensation in her stomach as he reached out to brush his fingers against her cheek before he drew her slowly towards him.

'Oh, I think so.' He tilted her head back. 'I could convince you.'

'No, I. . .' Her protest died as she sensed a tautening of his muscles before his face loomed closer. His warm breath fanned her cheek. She began to tremble uncontrollably as his lips brushed against hers, made a sweeping foray of her throat and back to her mouth.

The denial that hung on her lips was crushed. Instead, with a small sob of dismay, she gave herself up to the tide of emotions that flared out of control. She reached up, her fingers tangling in his dark hair, to draw him closer.

Even with Paul it had never been like this, this calculated plundering of her senses. Nothing had prepared her, either physically or mentally, for the riot of sensations this man was causing, or her own reaction to them.

She was shocked and appalled. What was she doing? What was she thinking of, giving in to the sheer sexual tension this man had so expertly, so ruthlessly contrived? What did she know about him, except that he seemed to be able to charm the birds from the trees? Well, she wasn't about to become a victim.

'No, please,' she said raggedly, pushing against him. His breath seemed to come unevenly as he released her. It needed an effort of will to keep her voice even.

'Satisfied, Doctor?'

His mouth twisted. 'I hate to disappoint you, Thea, but it would take more than one kiss.'

She almost choked on the idea of what other possibilities might spring to his devious mind. 'I don't know precisely what it was supposed to prove.' She swallowed hard. 'I don't even care. But from now on I'd prefer it if you kept your distance. In fact,' she said decisively, 'it would be better if, in future, you dealt with Andrew if you have any queries about Wellie.'

'I think you may just be overlooking something,' he cautioned, and she stared at him, swallowing hard. Why did she get the feeling that she may have won the battle but he wasn't about to concede the war?

'I don't see. . .'

'There's the small matter of the piece of land.'

'Land?'

'The piece of land on which you keep that. . .menagerie of yours.'

Thea stared at him. 'I have a lease, and before you start getting any ideas about moving boundaries,' she challenged hotly, 'let me assure you that my tenancy was a long-standing arrangement with Bob. In fact,' she added with a note of triumph, 'it still has six months to run.'

'Unfortunately it's no longer quite that simple. It may have escaped your notice, but things have changed. The land did belong to Bob. With his death it became my property and, as I'm sure you'll appreciate, land is a valuable asset.'

She chewed at her lip. 'Just what are you trying to say?'

His dark brows rose. 'I'm simply pointing out that I may have another use for that particular field. It would make very valuable building land, for instance.'

'Building. . .' The word was torn from her. 'You couldn't. You wouldn't.'

'I didn't say so. I'm merely pointing out the possibilities.'

'And money is, of course, a consideration,' she jibed.

'It certainly isn't something to be dismissed out of hand.'

Her lips parted on a gasp of dismay. 'But you can't do that.'

'I assure you, I can and will, unless you agree to abide by our existing arrangement. I happen to find it convenient. It suits me to have it continue. The choice is, of course, yours.'

A shiver ran along her spine. 'That's blackmail.'

'I'd prefer to call it a mutually beneficial arrangement.' A faint smile tugged at his lips. 'I'm not so easy to avoid, Thea. Like it or not, I'm here and I intend to stay, even if it makes waves in your cosy little set-up. The sooner you start getting used to the idea, the better.'

CHAPTER SEVEN

WHEN Thea had finally fallen asleep, it was to dream of a dark-cloaked figure, grinning fiendishly as he chased her across a field, and each time she had thought escape was in sight, it was only to discover that someone had moved the gate.

She had woken feeling exhausted and hollow-eyed and, as a result of her tossing and turning, there were shadows beneath her eyes, and her face when she looked in the mirror was so pale that she resorted to a hint of blusher on her cheeks before making her way with uncharacteristic reluctance to the surgery.

For once, her mind was anywhere but on her work. With six months of her lease to run and no chance of renewing it, even had she wanted to, which she had decided she didn't, she was faced with the problem of having to find an alternative site for the refuge or of having to let the animals go to new homes, always assuming, of course, that she could find them.

Two spots of angry colour had settled in her cheeks by the time she walked through Reception and into the consulting-room. Damn Joel Forrester!

Sandra looked up from the pile of cards she had just checked, her welcoming smile turning to a frown as Thea dropped her bag and sat motionless for a few seconds at the desk.

'Are you OK?'

'What? Oh, yes, sorry, I'm fine.' Thea forced herself to concentrate on the list of patients already awaiting her attention.

'You look a bit peaky. I hope you're not going in for this flu that's doing the rounds. Perhaps you ought to see a doctor.'

Thea took a steadying breath as she reached for the

cards. 'I'll be fine. Too many late nights, that's all.' With an effort, she tore her mind back from the memory of a punishing kiss, feeling her colour rise as she made a business of slipping into her clean, white coat. She looked pointedly at her watch. 'Shall we make a start? It sounds like bedlam out there.'

Sandra took the silently offered cue. 'Right,' she smiled. 'Prepare to repel boarders. Mr Payne's in with that old English sheepdog of his again.'

Thea stabbed her pen into her pocket and fixed a smile on her face. 'OK, let's do it. Right, Mr Payne, and how is Timmy this morning?'

'Well, he doesn't seem too good.' Joe Payne wrestled with several stones of energetic animal which collapsed, panting, at his feet. 'Can't exactly put my finger on it.'

'Let's take a look.' With Joe Payne helping to restrain his pet, Thea did a careful examination of the dog's glands, eyes and feet. 'Well they all seem fine,' she smiled. 'He doesn't seem to be in pain at all.' Her hands moved over the thick coat and the dog gazed at her with a mournful expression, his tongue licking briefly at her hand before he resumed his panting.

'I'll just check his throat. You never know, he may have a bit of an infection or swallowed a piece of bone which may have caused some scratches. They can get a bit uncomfortable. Let's have a look, Timmy. No, don't eat the light, silly old thing.'

The dog hauled himself to his feet, pushed himself against her and sank down again with a sigh. 'Well his throat seems fine, too. Is he eating properly?'

Joe Payne gave a wry laugh. 'He never stops. Eats us out of house and home, nearabouts.'

Nodding thoughtfully, Thea reached for her stethoscope. 'And what about exercise?'

'He's not so keen these days,' Joe said. 'I suppose he's getting on a bit, well, it comes to all of us, sooner or later.' He put an arm round the dog's shaggy neck. 'We're both slowing down a bit these days, aren't we, old fellow?'

Thea looked from the pensioner to the dog. 'How long have you had him, Joe? It can't be more than about six years?'

'Aye, something like that. But that's getting on a bit in dog years, isn't it?'

Thea laughed. 'It's not so ancient. Timmy should really be in the prime of his life.' She sobered slightly. 'Do you take him out for walks?'

'Oh, sure. I need the exercise myself, since I retired, but the old fellow seems to have taken against it lately. He starts off bright enough, but then he'll stop and lie down, as if he's had enough. It's not like him. We used to walk for miles along the coast road and over the fields.'

'He's not coughing at all?'

'No.' Joe Payne scratched his head. 'Honestly, I'm baffled.' He looked anxiously at Thea as she looped up the stethoscope and dropped it on to the table. 'You don't think. . .it's not something serious, is it?'

She smiled and shook her head. 'No, I'm sure it isn't. At least, not yet. But it could be.'

'How do you mean?' He looked distressed.

She ruffled the dog's coat. 'He's overweight, Sam. Basically he's eating too much and not getting enough exercise. It's a vicious circle. The more he eats the less he wants to run around, the less he runs around, the more weight he piles on.'

'But he only gets more or less what he always had. Except —' Joe's gaze narrowed thoughtfully '— well, I suppose we have started feeding him more of our own leftovers, scraps and all that, instead of that there manufactured stuff. It's cheaper, you see, since we retired, and old Timmy seems to love it.'

Thea said, 'Yes, I'm sure he does and I can't say I blame him.' Her eyes sparkled. 'I've sampled some of your Mabel's cooking. I know how good it is. Timmy's no fool, Joe. He must think he's living in a four-star hotel. But I'm afraid it's got to stop.' She smiled sympathetically. 'I know it won't be easy but, for

Timmy's sake, you've got to cut down on his rations. No titbits between meals, in fact one meal a day. Plenty of vegetables, pasta, no extra little treats. It's for his own good and I'm sure you'll find the results are worth it.'

Armed with a diet sheet, Joe and Timmy went on their way and Thea prepared for her next patient.

There were the routine booster injections against kennel cough and parvo virus. A cat needed his teeth scaling, followed by a budgie whose beak had to be clipped. Another dog, a Labrador this time, who needed a course of steroids for an arthritic condition, a goldfish with a fungal infection, and finally surgery was over, by which time Thea's head was well and truly aching.

It was with a sigh of relief that she saw Sandra come in carrying a large mug of steaming coffee. 'Oh, you're an angel.'

'I thought perhaps you could use these too.' Grinning, she proffered two aspirins.

'Even better.' Thea swallowed them gratefully, draining her coffee before slipping out of her white coat. 'I hardly dare ask how many calls there are.'

'As a matter of fact you're in luck.'

Thea stared at her. 'You mean. . .'

'Ssh, don't tempt fate. You're off this afternoon, aren't you?'

'That's right, and I can't say I'm sorry.' Thea completed her notes, frowning as the sound of the telephone ringing in Reception jangled her nerves.

'Lucky for some. How are you coping with old Mrs Pemberton's animals, by the way? I think it was awfully brave of you to take them on.'

'It's not so bad. A bit of a squeeze,' Thea agreed, scrawling her signature at the bottom of a letter before handing it to the girl. 'Could you give that to Karen to post on your way out.'

'Will do.' Sandra pocketed the envelope. 'So how do you manage for space?'

Thea pulled a face. 'It's a tight fit but, hopefully, Maggie won't be in hospital for too long. The problem is, she's getting on. How many more winters is she going to be able to manage alone up there? What happens to the animals when she finally decides to call it a day?'

Sandra half sat on the desk. 'You wouldn't be able to take them on a permanent basis?'

'Unfortunately it's not that simple. Oh, it would be difficult anyway.' Thea stared briefly out of the window before returning her attention to the desk. 'I've only a limited amount of space. But that isn't the problem.' Seeing Sandra's questioning gaze, she sighed heavily. 'The truth is, I've only six months left to run on my lease.'

'Well, surely that's no problem? Can't you just renew it the same as always?'

Thea gave a short laugh. 'It's a nice idea but I'm afraid this time it won't work that way. If you remember, the land doesn't belong to Bob any more.'

Sandra frowned. 'Well, no, but does it make any difference? I mean, his nephew. . .'

'I'm afraid Dr Forrester apparently has other plans.' She frowned, probing at the dull ache in her temple. 'I gather he sees the land in terms of an investment.' She couldn't bring herself to look at the other girl. 'It seems that he could get a very good price for it if he. . .if he sells it as building land?'

'You're not serious?' Sandra stared in disbelief. 'But surely he can't do that? I mean. . .he wouldn't, would he? Can you do things like that?'

Thea ran a distracted hand through her hair. 'Dr Forrester seems to be a law unto himself. I'm only just beginning to realise what he might be capable of. He's certainly not the sort of man who'd let a few animals stand in his way.' She swallowed hard. 'He's the most arrogant, self-opinionated man I've ever met.'

Sandra's hands hovered over the filing cabinet. 'Are you sure? I mean, it seems strange that I haven't heard anything and you could hardly keep that sort of thing quiet around here.' She shook her head. 'It's funny, I haven't seen much of him, of course, but he struck me as being really nice. Several of our clients have said how kind he is.'

'Yes, well, that only goes to show how easily he can fool them,' Thea said sharply. She looked up as someone tapped at the door and Karen popped her head round.

'Sorry to interrupt, Thea, but there's a call for you.'

Thea groaned. 'I knew it had to be too good to be true.' She looked at her watch. 'I don't suppose Andrew. . .?'

'Sorry, I did try. I know it's your afternoon off but he's asking to speak to you personally.'

'He?'

'Yes, it's Dr Forrester. He says it's urgent.'

'Speak of the devil,' Sandra muttered, waving as she made a hasty retreat. 'I'll leave you to it.'

Thea's lips compressed as she swept up a pile of case cards and said briskly, 'I'll come through to Reception and take it there.' She followed the other girl and picked up the phone. 'Yes.'

'Thea, is that you?'

It was ridiculous. Even the sound of his voice was sufficient to set her nerve-ends tingling. 'What do you want?'

'Can you come over?'

She drew a deep breath. If he imagined for one moment that just because he held the whip hand he simply had to call for her to come running, then he was in for a nasty shock. 'I'm afraid I do happen to be rather busy, Dr Forrester.' She had to turn away as Sandra pulled a face. 'Perhaps if you'd care to make an appointment?'

'Thea. . .?'

Her fingers tightened on the receiver. 'I thought I'd made it perfectly clear that I have no wish to see. . .'

'This isn't a social call, Thea.' His voice sounded rough edged with tension. 'It's Wellie.'

She froze, swallowing hard. 'What. . .? What's wrong?'

'I'm not sure but he's not looking too good. I think he's had some sort of relapse. I'd bring him to the surgery, but. . .'

'No.' She was thinking rapidly. 'It's best you don't move him, at least until I've had a chance to look at him and we know what the problem is.' She glanced up at the clock. 'Look, I'll be there as soon as possible. In the meantime try to keep him calm. Talk to him, but don't offer him anything to eat or drink.'

'Anything I can help with?' Andrew stood in the doorway as she put down the phone.

She turned to look at him. 'That was Joel. It sounds as if Wellie might have taken a turn for the worse.'

He frowned. 'In that case, you go. Don't worry about finishing up here. I'll handle any stragglers or calls.'

'Oh, bless you.' She was already reaching for her bag.

The drive from the practice to Joel's cottage took barely ten minutes. As she drove up, coming to a halt on the gravel drive, the door was already open. Hurrying in, she heard Joel call.

'Thea? We're in the kitchen.'

She found him kneeling beside the dog, stroking its head. She went down swiftly beside him, opening her bag and reaching for a stethoscope. 'Has there been any change?'

Glancing up he moved aside for her to make an examination. He looked tired, as if he hadn't slept. He shook his head. 'He's about the same. He looks as if he's in shock.'

'Let's take a look. Hello, Wellie, old chap.' Speaking softly, Thea applied the stethoscope to the dog's chest, listening intently. 'Mm, that's certainly banging away at a rate of knots. The pulse-rate must be at least one hundred and forty.' Frowning, she ran a hand over the animal's skin and legs before checking his eyes and mouth. 'His temperature is low. His pupils are dilated too.'

She straightened up, dropping the stethoscope into her bag. Joel rose to his feet beside her.

'How is he?'

'He's pretty sick.' She forced herself to meet his gaze. 'You can see that for yourself.'

'It's not the chest infection, though?'

She shook her head. 'No. I'm afraid all the signs point to a heart attack.'

'I thought as much.' Joel's voice rasped a little.

'You look awful. Did you get any sleep last night?'

'Not much.'

'I thought not.'

He raked a hand through his hair. 'Is there anything we can do?'

'You can find a blanket. We need to keep him warm.'

Joel disappeared upstairs. By the time he returned she had checked that Wellie's airway was clear and made him as comfortable as possible.

'What are we going to do?' He draped the blanket over the semi-conscious animal.

Thea said quietly, 'I won't insult you by pretending there's an easy answer. You must know the odds. A heart attack isn't good, especially not in a dog of Wellie's age.'

'I'm a doctor,' he advised hardly. 'You don't need to spell it out.' He swore softly under his breath. 'Hell, I didn't mean to say that.'

Almost involuntarily, she placed a hand on his arm. 'You don't need to apologise. I know how worried you are, how much Wellie means to you.' She felt his muscles tauten.

'You're doing your job. I'm over-reacting. Do whatever you have to do.'

'I can't give any guarantees, you know that?'

He nodded, his mouth tightening. 'This is crazy. It's just a dog.'

'Not just a dog,' Thea said gently. 'Wellie was never that. He's a part of all our lives and we're not about to give up on him.'

Slowly he let her go. 'Just tell me what you want me to do?'

'Normally I'd move him to the surgery, but, if you have no objection, I'd like to take him to my place instead.'

'You don't have to do that, you know. I could probably do anything that needs doing.'

And it might make life a whole lot easier if she let him. The thought was banished the instant it rose. 'I'm sure you could, but I'm the vet around here,' she reminded him evenly, and saw his eyes narrow.

'You mean you can deal cold-heartedly with it? More dispassionately.'

Right now, she thought, her heart was feeling decidedly fragile. He looked tired and defeated and it needed an effort of will not to wrap her arms around him and kiss the tension from his mouth. This was a side to Joel Forrester she hadn't seen before and it confused her.

'I hope I can be professional and objective,' she said softly. 'If you think about it, it makes sense. The last thing I need right now is for Wellie to become excited. If he sees you he'll want to play or expect to be taken for a walk, even if he is feeling ill. Besides, that way I can keep a close eye on him.'

She reached for her bag. 'I'm going to give him an injection, something to steady his heart, then it might be a good idea if we move him so that he has time to settle and get used to different surroundings before it gets dark. We'll wait until it's had time to take effect then perhaps you can lift him into the Land Rover.'

Wellie lay, unprotesting, as she inserted the needle gently beneath the skin. 'The best thing for him now is sleep,' she said, straightening up.

Joel knelt to stroke the silky fur. 'You're right; I think he's already resting more easily.'

Thea stared at his broad back, the wide shoulders

and lean hips, her mind unfocused until he straightened up. 'I'll make some tea.' She half turned but his hand closed over her wrist and she was shaken by the riot of sensations that coursed through her.

'Thea, wait.' He held her hand, kissed the palm. 'Trust me, Thea.'

Easily said. Swallowing hard, her gaze skittered away from his.

His gaze narrowed. She heard his sharp intake of breath as he moved closer. Her eyes closed as his mouth came down on hers, a strange new kind of awareness bringing the faint colour to her cheeks.

She was appalled by her own weakness where he was concerned. What about Paul? The voice of her conscience stirred. She said hoarsely, 'Joel, no. I. . .' But her plea went unheeded as he drew her closer, his hand effortlessly dealing with the buttons of her blouse. Her breath caught in her throat as his fingers sought and found the curved fullness of her breast. She groaned softly.

'I don't want to be your enemy, Thea,' he murmured before his mouth found hers again, seeking out its sweet moistness.

She didn't want to be his enemy either. That was the trouble — she didn't know what she wanted. Her head was telling her one thing but her heart wasn't listening. Didn't she owe some kind of loyalty to Paul? But she had never felt this way with Paul, never felt desire flare out of control.

'You're driving me crazy, you know that?' Joel groaned against her hair, the deepening kiss rousing her to a state of longing she had never experienced before. Moaning softly, she swayed towards him. Her breath caught in her throat, then her hands rose to his neck, tangling in the thick darkness of his hair. He drew her closer until it seemed their bodies merged with a force of energy that was almost frightening.

She felt him tense as he raised his head. She was

aware of his blue eyes darkening, then he set her free,
his breathing harsh as he drew away.

'Joel. I saw the car outside. I'm so glad I caught you.'

Only then, as the door swung slowly open, was Thea
aware of Joel deliberately shielding her from view,
giving her time to fumble with the buttons on her
blouse as he spoke to the figure standing in the doorway. She swept a hand through her hair, guessing how
she must look.

'I'm sorry I let myself in, only the door was open.'
Helen Crawford's smiling gaze went beyond him to
Thea's flushed face and her mouth tightened fractionally. 'Oh, it's Miss Somers, isn't it? I do hope I haven't
caught you at an inconvenient moment?'

'No, of course not.'

Their responses came simultaneously. Thea straightened her shoulders, wishing uncomfortably that she
could be anywhere else but here as she avoided the
sardonic gleam in Joel's eyes. It was galling to see him
looking so unflustered.

'I was just about to leave anyway,' she said. 'I just
have to collect my bag.'

Pansy-brown eyes concentrated on Joel again. 'I was
on my way back to the surgery to leave a message,
asking if you could possibly find time to call and see
Mrs Walker, up at Willowtree Farm? She had her baby
early this morning.'

'Yes, of course. This is her third, isn't it?'

'That's right. It was a perfectly straightforward delivery but she was in labour for quite a while so she's
pretty exhausted, and the baby has a touch of jaundice.
I'm sure it's nothing to worry about.'

'It's no problem. I'll make time to get out there later
this afternoon,' he said.

'It's so nice to have you back in circulation,' Helen
smiled, her voice softly lilting. 'I can't wait to hear all
about Canada. We must get together and have a long
chat.'

'Yes, we must. I've a lot of catching up to do myself.'

Thea watched, fascinated, as a faint blush gathered in the other woman's cheeks as she slipped a hand through his arm. Like someone staking her claim, Thea thought, conscious of her shaking hands as she coiled the stethoscope and dropped it into her bag.

'I've often thought I might spread my own wings a bit,' Helen was saying. 'I've heard Canada is full of opportunities, not to mention those huge brown bears.' Her girlish giggle grated on Thea's nerves and she snapped the locks on her bag far more sharply than was necessary. 'I've heard they can be terribly dangerous.'

'I didn't see any bears.' Glinting blue eyes suddenly levelled with Thea's. 'In any case, I can promise you, there are far more dangerous creatures than bears around here. The only difference is that they come small and sweet, and they strike when you least expect it. Isn't that right, Thea?'

She straightened her shoulders, with an effort keeping her voice even. 'Yes, well, I wouldn't know about that.' She reached for her bag. 'If you don't mind, I'd like to get Wellie settled for the night. I'd like to keep an eye on him at my place, if you have no objection?'

'Of course not. I'll carry him out to the Land Rover.'

'There's no need. . .'

'I'll do it, Thea.' He raised a mocking eyebrow and she felt the colour flare into her cheeks. 'I'm sure Helen won't mind waiting?'

Thea followed as he carried Wellie out, wrapped in a blanket and gently closed the door of the vehicle. 'I'll call you in the morning.'

She half turned away, fumbling for her keys. 'You don't have to do that. If there's any change I'll let you know.'

'Thea.' He drew her gently towards him. 'I haven't thanked you.'

Why couldn't he just let her go? She gasped softly then as his mouth came down on hers.

'Goodbye, Thea. Sleep tight.'

Fat chance, she thought, as her heart gave an extra

thud. At this rate she would be lucky if she ever slept again.

It was only later, when she realised she had read the same page of the local paper twice without having taken in a single word, that Thea drew herself up briskly and marched into the kitchen where she proceeded to tie back her hair, donned an apron and reached for her washing up gloves.

She turned the tap on full and scrubbed furiously at a dish she had earlier left in soak. It was ridiculous to allow one simple kiss to affect her in such a way, except that, when she thought about that kiss, her cheeks still burned. She emptied the last of the crockery out of the cupboard, slamming it with unaccustomed fury on to the kitchen surface.

This wasn't the way she had planned to spend her afternoon off, but, when it came to it, she hadn't been able to relax. An hour later, sitting wearily in the kitchen, waiting for some soup to heat, she stifled a tiny groan of dismay as Paul's car pulled up outside.

'It's OK, it's official,' he explained, kissing her cheek. 'I'm off duty.'

'I'm glad to hear it,' said Thea drily, automatically reaching for another dish.

'What's this?'

'Tomato soup.' A spoon clattered on to the table. 'It's been a hectic day. Some of us didn't get any lunch.'

Paul pulled a face. 'Mm, very nice, but I was rather hoping for something a little better. I thought you might like to go somewhere for a nice meal.'

'Why?'

'Does there have to be a reason?' His face assumed a vaguely pained expression.

Guilty conscience, maybe? She dismissed the thought as uncharitable, and raked a hand through her hair. 'I'm sorry, Paul, but, do you mind if we give it a miss? It really has been a bad day. I feel an absolute mess and, to be honest, I'd quite like an early night.'

There was an almost imperceptible pause before he

said in a voice tinged very slightly with annoyance, 'You don't mind me dropping in, do you? I suppose I should have rung, but I didn't think you'd mind.' He turned her to face him, grinning wryly. 'What's the matter? Is my boyish charm starting to fade?'

'Oh, Paul, for heaven's sake,' Thea heard herself snap the words, while supposing guiltily that perhaps it was becoming a habit. She was on the brink of relenting, except that, for once, she genuinely did want a quiet evening and an early night.

He looked hurt and her voice softened as she felt a swift rush of affection for him. 'I really am sorry. I shouldn't have snapped at you like that. It's just. . . Wellie's taken a turn for the worse. I think he's had a slight heart attack.'

'Oh, is that all? You silly goose.' He pulled her into his arms. 'Why didn't you say? I was beginning to think it was something personal.'

She stiffened. 'I happen to be very fond of Wellie.'

'Yes of course you are, my sweet.' He laughed but she sensed a faint note of irritation in his voice. 'You don't have to explain. I'm disappointed, of course, but there will be other times.'

'Yes, of course there will.' She deliberately drove a note of cheerfulness into her voice. 'Tomorrow perhaps?'

'No, not tomorrow. I've — er, I've promised my services to the local darts committee.'

Was his response almost too quick? Too pat? She wondered, briefly, if he was trying to give her a taste of her own medicine. If so, she guessed he would have been shocked to know that all she felt was relief at the prospect of a couple of free nights. She purposely kept her voice bland.

'Oh, well, it can't be helped, I suppose.' She turned away.

'Thea——' Paul caught her hand, turning her to face him and stared at her fingers. 'We've had some good times together, haven't we?'

She smiled. 'Yes, of course we have.' With an uneasy premonition she guessed what was coming and wished he hadn't chosen now.

'You know how fond I am of you? I know we're not exactly engaged, and that's probably my fault.' He looked at her and must have seen the sudden look of wary resistance in her eyes. 'It's not that I didn't care enough. Quite the contrary. Thea, you must know that some day I'd thought. . .hoped. . .'

She stared at him unhappily, searching desperately for something to say. 'Oh, Paul.'

'I've always thought. . .hoped you felt the same way.'

Thea was conscious of a sudden tightness in her throat. A month ago she would have been so sure. But now? 'I'm very fond of you too.'

His mouth twisted. 'I was rather hoping for something more than just fond. This can't have come as any surprise.'

She shook her head. 'But I thought we were both happy with things the way they are. Why now?'

'Damn it, Thea! Is there ever a right time?' His jaw tightened. 'What do you suggest? A week from now, a month? A year?' He suddenly looked like a spoilt child. 'Well, you may as well know, I don't see my life going on the way it is forever. I'd like to know where I stand.'

She swallowed hard. 'I don't understand.'

'There's no future for me here in this God-forsaken backwater, Thea, that's been made pretty clear. Well, I need to know where I'm going, both personally and professionally. If I'm wasting my time, I'd rather know.'

She stared at him unhappily. 'Are you saying that I can influence your decision? This is some sort of ultimatum?' She saw the colour rise in his neck.

'There's not much to keep me here, Thea. I don't intend to spend the rest of my life playing second fiddle. I'm a good doctor in my own right, in spite of what Mr High and Mighty Forrester might think. There are places where I would be more highly regarded.' He gave a sharp laugh. 'I could earn more.'

He swore impatiently then looked away. 'You have to know some time—it may as well be now. I've been toying with the idea of going abroad. I've applied for several jobs. I think there's a pretty good chance I might be offered one of them and I need to know. . .if it comes to it, would you be willing to come with me?'

She drew in a deep breath. 'You're asking me to marry you?'

He seemed oddly discomfited. 'That too, of course. We'd need to get settled. But I need to know where I stand, Thea. I have my future to consider.'

And what about my future? The thought refused to be pushed away as she stared at him. 'Yes, of course.' In a way she almost felt sorry for him. They were both on edge for some reason. Whatever the cause, she felt too weary to argue. Maybe this was her fault. She should have seen it coming. Her feelings for Paul, once apparently so clear, suddenly seemed too vague and insubstantial. Maybe if she hadn't let things drift.

'Where exactly——' she moistened her dry lips with her tongue '—where were you thinking of going?'

He shrugged. 'Australia, New Zealand, maybe. Doctors are always appreciated out there.'

Australia. She swallowed hard. 'Oh, Paul. I'm so sorry. I just wasn't expecting any of this. I don't know what to say.'

'Is it so difficult to come to a decision about our future together?'

'But don't you see, that's just the point,' she tried to reason. 'My life is here. I enjoy my work. I like living in a small community. I like the people.'

'It's a backwood, Thea. Nothing changes. It's like living in a time warp.'

'Maybe that's what suits me,' she snapped wearily and then relented. 'I'm fond of you, Paul, very fond.' Instinctively she reached out to touch his hand. 'But don't you see marriage is a big commitment? It's not the sort of contract I would feel could ever be broken and. . .going abroad, leaving all my friends behind. . .'

Ungraciously he drew away from her. 'If you mean one friend in particular,' he suggested snidely, 'then let me tell you, you're on a loser. Forrester isn't the marrying sort. Once bitten, twice shy, Thea. Isn't that what they say?'

She had to swallow hard to get rid of the lump in her throat as she said quietly, 'I don't know what you mean?'

'No?' He laughed. 'Didn't you know? Well then let me be the one to break the news. Forrester was married.'

CHAPTER EIGHT

FOR A second, Thea imagined the ground had shifted beneath her feet.

'I had no idea. You said *was* married.'

'That's right. It seems he met her while he was in medical school. She was a dancer or something, ballet, something like that.' Paul laughed scornfully. 'Anyway, it seems she soon realised what she had let herself in for. He expected her to settle down here. Can you imagine it? Giving up London and showbiz to be a doctor's wife?'

'You mean she left him?' Thea enquired, helpless against the need to know.

'Oh, no. It seems, after he qualified, he came back here to go into partnership with Bob. At least, that was the plan. It lasted three months, then, apparently, she decided she couldn't stand the boredom any longer so she upped and left, heading back to her friends, and who can blame her? Once the divorce came through, Forrester took off overseas.' Paul's hand closed over hers. 'So you see, he may be back, Thea, but he's not likely to want to get involved again, not seriously, anyway.'

The information shocked Thea. It explained so much, most of all why Joel was such a loner. She said quietly, 'He must have had a bad time.'

'Don't waste your sympathy on Forrester,' Paul said. 'His sort use women, Thea. He enjoys being a big fish in a small pool. Don't get hooked. You're not in his league.'

She shook her head, conscious of the sudden tightness in her throat, wondering whether she had imagined the faint note of satisfaction in Paul's voice.

She used the boiling kettle as an excuse to draw away

and was annoyed to discover, as she poured water on to instant coffee, that her hands were trembling. Doubts tore at her, making her head throb with dull pain. It certainly explained a lot, she had to admit. That faint air of cynicism, the apparent lack of any firm relationship or roots in Joel's life. His sole commitment was to his work. Beyond that, what did she really know about him?

She had told herself his kisses must mean something, but what if she was wrong? Was she just a challenge to his male ego? Was that how he saw her?

She needed to think clearly and that wasn't easy when she felt as if she was being pulled in opposite directions. She placed two mugs of coffee on the table. 'I need more time to make a decision about something that affects my whole future, Paul.'

'How much time?'

'I don't know.' She stared at him unhappily, and it was almost like looking at a stranger. 'How soon do you need to know?'

'Probably within the next six weeks.'

'Six weeks!' She looked at him and said slowly, 'And if I decide I can't go with you?'

'I'd prefer it if we were together, Thea, but it's your choice.'

She passed her tongue over her dry lips. 'Oh, Paul, I'm sorry. It's just that. . . I don't seem to be able to think straight. This has all come as a bit of a shock. I need time to think.'

His mouth tightened. 'I hadn't realised it would need so much thought.'

'You're asking me to give up quite a lot.' She moved towards the door, held it open. 'If you don't mind, I'd really like to be alone right now.'

Surprise flared briefly in his eyes before he followed her to the door. Outside, it was beginning to get dark. 'I'll call you, Thea.'

She nodded. 'I promise, I'll think about it, but not right now. I'm too tired; I need a clear head.'

Ungraciously he refused to look at her. Maybe she shouldn't blame him, not when, in her own heart, she harboured the suspicion that if she really did love Paul she wouldn't have needed to think about it at all.

Several days later, Thea drew back the bedroom curtains, on the morning of the spring fête, and viewed the bright morning with mixed feelings.

'Someone up there doesn't like me,' she confided in Jess as the collie padded after her into the kitchen, where she flipped the switch on the kettle and made herself coffee and a piece of toast.

Stifling a yawn, she carried her cup and plate to sit with her arms propped on the table, savouring her first coffee of the day and looked with disgust at the brilliant sunshine splashing rays of light on to the floor.

'I spend the night praying for rain and look what happens. You're right, I shouldn't complain.' She fed a crust to Jess, whose tail thudded joyfully against the floor. 'And you needn't look so smug. It's a diet for you, my girl,' she warned, a rueful smile tugging at her lips. 'Oh, well, it looks as if I'm just going to have to put up with a fête worse than death. I suppose I should be grateful it's only once a year.'

Piling her crockery into the sink, she went to rescue the morning post from the mat, skimming through the buff-coloured envelopes before dispatching them into the bin. 'Right, time I looked at our first patient, I think. Oh, you're coming too, are you? Just behave then. Wellie's not ready to start playing quite yet.'

Collecting her stethoscope from her bag and with the collie at her heels, Thea went into the sitting-room to where Wellie lay sprawled in a large basket.

'OK, so how are you feeling today then? You certainly look brighter.' She listened intently to the reassuring thud of a much steadier heartbeat before straightening up. 'Yes, you're definitely getting better, aren't you?'

She stroked the big, dark head. 'But not well enough yet for walks. You're going to have to stay where you are for a while yet.' Not that the dog seemed to mind as, with a soft hrumph of pleasure, he took the proffered tablet from her hand and settled down, content to watch as Thea busied herself, moving from room to room, generally making a start on her day.

Free of the routine of surgeries on alternate weekends, Saturdays were usually her day for catching up on chores and shopping, and, hopefully, finding time to relax.

'Fat chance of that today,' she muttered, rinsing the dishes. If there was one thing she could have done without, it was to find herself roped into judging bonny, bouncing babies. Damn Joel Forrester! she thought, scouring a pan with far greater vigour than it warranted.

With an effort she hauled her thoughts back to safer practicalities. There was still work to be done before she showered and changed for the fête, which was due officially to be opened at midday. If she was ever going to be ready it was time she got herself organised and made a start on the list of things still to be done.

Half an hour later, wearing jeans and a bright red sweater, feet tucked into a pair of green wellingtons, she was out in the paddock, feeding and checking the animals.

Maggie Pemberton's cats, in their run, came to greet her as she carried in bowls of fresh food and water, rubbing against her ankles, purring loudly. 'Yes, I'm pleased to see you too,' she stroked and played with each one in turn. 'Maggie will be home soon, then you'll get all the fuss you want.'

Moving on to the cages, Barney, as always, treated her visits with disdain, turning his head to stare at her with large amber eyes. 'Well you're certainly looking much better,' she said in amusement, having checked the damaged wing. 'A few more days, just to be on the safe side, and you can be released. What do you think of that then?' Barney clearly wasn't impressed. 'I'm not surprised,' she smiled, running the back of her finger against his chest. 'You're getting too comfortable for your own good.'

Thumper, on the other hand, was eager to take food from her hand and to have his ears fondled. 'All right, all right. Keep still,' she admonished, lifting the rabbit to inspect the wound on his back leg. 'That's doing nicely too.' She placed him gently back in the hutch where he instantly set about burying himself in a heap of straw. 'At this rate I shall soon be redundant,' she told them all cheerfully, not believing it for one second.

'Dare I take that as a promise?' The clear, well-modulated voice coming from behind her sent her whirling to face Joel, spilling a dish of water in the process as for an instant her breath caught in her throat. He was dressed casually yet smartly, his shirt open at the neck, fawn trousers and matching jacket.

'Damn! Now look what you made me do. Do you have to creep up on people like that?' She brushed ineffectually at the damp patch on her jeans, lowering her head in an attempt to hide the sudden rise of colour in her cheeks.

'I didn't creep. You were so busy talking to yourself, you didn't hear me coming.' His gaze surveyed the neat rows of cages and their various occupants. 'I must say, they all look remarkably healthy.'

'Most of them are, now.'

'So you'll be planning to release them?'

'I'm afraid some of them will probably never go back into the wild,' she said defensively. Was he really so eager to close the refuge down in order to build some monstrosity? She shuddered at the unthinkable, then frowned. 'Aren't you a little early? The fête doesn't start until midday?'

'We did agree to meet up with the rest of the judges, half an hour before the official opening,' Joel pointed out.

Thea's gaze flew to her watch. 'Oh, no! I'd completely forgotten.'

He sighed heavily. 'Perhaps you'd better go and change? I'll finish up here.'

'Well. . . Just don't put your fingers anywhere near Claudia.' Claudia was a rather vicious parrot.

His face assumed a pained expression. 'Believe me, nothing would induce me to go within a yard of her.'

Their arrival at the show caused an immediate ripple of attention. A smiling Helen Crawford came towards them, hooking her hand possessively into Joel's arm, and he was immediately surrounded by a crowd of well-wishers, all welcoming him back into the friendly community, some, jokingly, asking did he intend to stay this time or was he just passing through?

Caught up in a huddle with the rest of those coerced into acting as judges, Thea was unable to catch his reply and bit her lips with frustration, forcing herself, with an effort, to pay attention to the lady in a large hat who was airing her views on the surprising range of home-made wines displayed on one of the tables.

After that, Thea was kept too busy casting a professional eye over the assembled ranks of babies of all shapes and sizes, some clearly resenting all the attention, and bestowing prizes, to have time to think too much about Joel.

Just occasionally she would catch a glimpse of his dark head as he mingled with the crowd, chatting with people of all age-groups, but he was never so far away that she could not be aware of him, throwing back his head and laughing, deeply engaged in conversation.

She tore her gaze away and caught a fleeting glimpse of Paul, chatting avidly to a girl she recognised vaguely, before the pair of them disappeared into one of the refreshment tents.

The event was going well. The local people had turned out in full force, as well as outsiders, drawn by what had proved to be a popular yearly event. The weather helped, too, Thea thought, brushing the back of her hand across her forehead as the sun continued to shine from a near-cloudless sky. She was glad she had chosen to wear the white trousers with the navy and white, sailor-type top and a light blazer, just in case it became chilly later in the afternoon.

Thea handed out the last trophy with a smile for the mother of the winner, posing for a photograph for the local paper. Her own duties complete, she lifted the heavy swathe of auburn hair from her neck with a sigh and looked with longing at the crowded beer tent. It was too busy to fight her way through. Instead she made for the ice-cream van and came away clutching two giant-sized cones.

Joel was bestowing the final award and a kiss to the winner of the best cake. He bent to pick up a small child, posing for a photograph. It was surprising, that odd little jerk her heart gave at the sight of him, so tall and dark, nursing the golden-haired infant who beamed, one finger stuck in her mouth before she reached out for Joel's ear.

Thea watched him hand the child back to its mother before moving in her direction.

'I thought you might be glad of some refreshment.' She held out the cone and he viewed it with relieved anticipation.

'You're a lifesaver. Come on, let's get out of here and find a quiet spot with some shade.' His hand was under her arm and he was propelling her towards a row of trees at the edge of the field.

'Won't we be missed?' She licked the edges of the cone, relishing the milky sweetness.

'I shouldn't think so. We've done what was expected of us. I think we're entitled to relax and enjoy the rest of the afternoon in our own way, don't you?' His mouth twitched slightly. 'You have ice-cream on your face.' He reached out a hand, gently removing the droplet from her cheek. 'You look about twelve years old.'

But she didn't feel like a twelve-year-old! Her head jerked up and, as if he had been waiting for it, his mouth descended without warning over hers. She moaned softly as her body responded traitorously. I'm so weak, she thought, thoroughly spineless.

She gasped as his lips made a teasing foray over her eyes and cheek, nuzzling at her ear before returning to claim her mouth in a heated demand that banished every thought of resistance from her mind.

His hands moved to her hair, drawing her relentlessly closer, loosening the clips, and went on, remorselessly inviting responses which her body gave until she moaned softly. It was utterly crazy, but he seemed to have robbed her of the power to resist.

The spell was shattered as she found herself suddenly thrust away to stand shaking with confusion. Her hand flew to her mouth where the pressure of his lips still remained, and she felt the heat of her burning cheeks.

But as she looked at him she heard him make an odd sound in his throat and his expression changed. Her gaze followed his to look with rapt fascination at the contents of the ice-cream cone clinging stickily to the once crisp whiteness of his shirt and she heard the groan which escaped her own lips. She shook her head, making incoherent sounds.

'Don't,' he gritted. 'Just don't say a word.'

She had the feeling that if she had said a word he would cheerfully have strangled her with those hands which, only moments ago, had made her shiver with delight.

'I'm sorry.'

'Why is it that I only have to come within a hundred yards of you for the world to start falling around my ears?' he gritted. 'Since we met I've been attacked by a pile of boxes, almost broken my foot, come pretty close to having my car clamped. . .'

'We don't have clamps. . .'

'Don't push your luck,' he advised hardly. 'Since the minute I arrived you've done nothing but shatter my peace of mind. You and your damned animals have invaded my privacy. . .'

'They aren't *damned* animals,' she pointed out, outraged. Why were they arguing again? 'At least, for wild animals, they behave in a reasonably civil manner.'

'Civil!' His dark eyebrows rose. 'That paranoid maneating parrot wouldn't know civil if you fed it to him . . .her, coated in sugar.'

Her spine stiffened. 'Well, if you will stick your fingers in the cage, what can you expect?' she retorted sharply. 'I didn't ask to live next door to. . .to someone so. . .bigoted.'

'Bigoted!'

'And animal-hating and bad. . .'

She didn't get to finish. The breath in her body exploded in a sudden gasp as his hands clamped on to her arms, jerking her towards him, moulding her against his powerfully masculine frame.

'Why is it that I want to kiss you and throttle you all at the same time?' he growled. 'You're like a thorn under my skin, constantly irritating, so much so, damn it, that I notice when you're not there.'

He didn't move and Thea looked up at him, bemused, uncomprehending, then he bent his head and with slow deliberation began to kiss her again. A shudder of desire racked her body.

'You must know how much I want you,' he said thickly while his hands moved to caress her curves.

Suddenly he stiffened, pulling away, and she uttered a soft moan of protest. What had she done wrong?

He swore lightly under his breath and only then did she realise that they weren't alone.

'Oh, Dr Forrester, thank heavens I found you.' Jane Watts, chairman of the fête committee cast the briefest glance in Thea's direction. 'You're needed urgently in the first aid tent.'

'What's happened?' He was instantly all professional, Thea realised, an oppressive weight suddenly lodging in her chest as it seemed the gentleness of a few moments ago might never have happened.

'It's Bill Parker. He's collapsed. He looks pretty bad.'

'I'll be right there. Have you seen Paul, Dr Prescott?'

'I saw him earlier,' Thea said; 'he was going into the beer tent.'

'In that case you'd better come with me,' he advised hardly.

'But. . .'

'I may need your help, Thea. You know about animals. In an emergency, people are not so different.'

She nodded and set off across the field, suddenly wishing she was wearing more sensible shoes and her practical jeans. She stumbled and Joel's hand came firmly under her elbow, reawakening sensations she would far rather had lain dormant.

In the first aid tent, Bill Parker lay on the grass on someone's coat. He was about sixty years old, heavily built. His eyes were closed, his breathing was shallow and his face was pale and clammy. Thea felt her heart sink.

'Has anyone sent for an ambulance?' Joel rapped as he knelt to loosen the man's tie.

'It's on its way,' one of the young first-aiders said. 'We did what we could to make him comfortable.'

'Do you know exactly what happened?'

The girl shook her head. 'He just seemed to collapse suddenly, clutching at his arm.' She frowned. 'It's a heart attack, isn't it?'

'It certainly looks like it.' Joel had stripped off his jacket and was checking for the man's pulse. 'My medical bag is in the car.'

'I'll get it.' Thea took the keys and sped away, returning seconds later, to fling the bag open, extracting a stethoscope.

'Good girl,' Joel murmured softly before making a swift but thorough examination of the unconscious man. He finally straightened up, frowning. 'You said his name is Parker?'

The girl nodded. 'That's right. Bill Parker. He farms over at Trevannic. We don't see much of him in the village.'

'Damn! It might help if I knew a bit about him. Does he have any relatives?'

'No,' Thea answered, shaking her head. 'I know him, slightly. His wife died a couple of years back. He's been living alone on the farm since. I know because I had to go out to do a routine testing of his dairy herd about six months ago.'

Joel's face tightened. 'I suppose you wouldn't happen to know if he was taking any medication? If he had any history of heart trouble?'

Thea frowned then nodded. 'He did mention. . .yes, he was complaining that your uncle wanted him to see a specialist.' She smiled slightly. 'I don't think he held with doctors. He reckoned a good dose of fresh air could put most things to rights.'

'Yes, well this is one instance where he's going to need more specialist help. Hell!' Joel swore softly under his breath, moving quickly. 'Quick, he's arresting.'

Thea moved instinctively, tilting the man's head back, clearing the airway as Joel set up an immediate cardiac massage, one hand placed firmly over the other as he applied a firm but steady pressure in an attempt to restart Bill Parker's heart.

She could see the film of sweat glistening on Joel's brow as the seconds passed. He worked determinedly. 'One. . .two. . .three. . . Come on, dammit, breathe.'

'Let me take over for a while.'

He shook his head. 'I'm not getting a response. Try mouth-to-mouth.'

Thea breathed a steady flow of air into the man's lungs, feeling the steady rise of his chest. She was only vaguely aware of the tension around them, then the arrival of the ambulance and, finally, Joel's sharp grunt of satisfaction.

'I've got a pulse. Come on, man, breathe. That's it. You're going to be all right.' All the time he was talking, reassuring.

Thea rose weakly to her feet, making way for the paramedics.

'OK, Doc, we'll see to him now.'

She stood, waiting, as Joel told them what he knew about the man's background and what had happened. Then, at last, the ambulance was on its way. By now most people had begun to drift away from the field, leaving the few to clear up, stacking away tables and chairs, gathering up litter.

The early evening sun was cooler and a breeze helped to freshen the air. Thea lifted the heavy swathe of hair from her neck, realising that she was suddenly very tired.

'Come on, I'll take you home.'

'There's really no need. . .'

'Don't argue, Thea. It's been a long day. I need a shower and a long drink. Let's get out of here.'

It wasn't until the car coasted to a halt that she gathered her senses sufficiently to realise that they weren't at her cottage but at his.

'I want to put a call through to the hospital as quickly as possible,' he said. 'They'll need to know what happened and any treatment I gave. I know the ambulance crew were fully briefed, but I'll feel happier if I speak to David West myself since, officially, it looks as if I'm Bill Parker's GP.' He ran a hand through his hair. 'Why the devil didn't he come and see me?'

'Bill's the sort who doesn't like to put people out. Maybe he's been feeling all right.'

Joel tossed his jacket on to a nearby chair and Thea watched him, sensing the tension that was still in him. 'Pour some drinks.' He indicated the cabinet. 'You'll find some brandy. I know it's early but I could do with one. Make yourself at home. I'll make that call. I won't be long.'

He left her and Thea poured drinks, one large brandy and a smaller one for herself. Sipping at it, she took a long look around. It was a pleasant room. She had always liked it when Bob was alive but she could see where Joel had already begun to stamp his own person-ality on it in the rows of books, the few antiques dotted around, carefully chosen to add even more beauty to the room. A lamp, standing on the gleaming surface of a small, rosewood table, a large arrangement of dried flowers standing in the wide old fireplace. She fingered the petals.

'Not my work, I'm afraid.'

She hadn't heard him returning. She blushed, thinking he might imagine she had been prying. 'I'm sorry.'

'There's no need to apologise. I said make yourself at home. I meant it.' He had changed, she realised. He was wearing jeans and a fresh shirt. His hair looked slightly damp. 'Sorry to take so long.' He reached for his drink. 'I took a quick shower.'

His blue gaze skimmed over her and all at once she was painfully aware of the way she must look. Her shirt was sticky and creased, her hair dishevelled. With as much dignity as she could muster, she put her glass firmly on the table.

'Any news of Bill Parker?'

'It's a little too early to say. They're working on him. At least he's alive.'

'Thanks to you.'

'And to you.' He placed his own glass on the table.

She smiled slightly. 'I didn't do much.'

'That's not true.' He stood with his hands in his pockets, looking at her. 'Why didn't you go in for medicine? You'd have been good at it. You have the right temperament. You don't panic.'

'I did go in for medicine,' she reminded him, flushing slightly at the unexpected praise.

'I meant human beings, Thea—people.'

She shrugged slightly. 'Animals need caring for, too. In a way they're even more vulnerable than people. They can't tell you when they feel ill. They can only show you, in the way they behave.'

A spasm flickered across his features. She sensed a tautening of his muscles and found herself gazing in rapt fascination as his face suddenly loomed closer, bringing with it the utterly sensuous mouth.

He tilted her face, cupping it in his hands and said softly, 'I want you, Thea. God knows, I've tried to fight it, but it's no good. I want to make love to you. I want to hold you, to feel your body against mine. Don't go,' he said huskily. 'Stay here with me.'

The effect was as devastating as it was confusing. She was trembling too much to speak. 'I. . .' Her voice faltered. 'It isn't that I don't want to. It's just. . .'

His lips brushed against hers. 'Trust me, Thea.'

She wanted to, desperately. His hands tightened on her arms. He groaned softly as his mouth made feathering advances over her throat and eyes before returning to her mouth, claiming it with a passion that left them both breathless.

She responded with a ferocity that both surprised and shocked her as it matched his own. This was where she belonged, where she wanted to be. She could feel the powerful strength of his hands through the thin fabric of her blouse. A tiny, purely involuntary shiver of desire ran through her.

'Have you any idea how much I want you?' His mouth was close to her ear as he stroked her hair.

She moaned softly and he stared down at her, breathing unevenly. 'God, I want you so much,' he murmured raggedly.

'I want you too,' she said huskily. She swayed, her head going back, her eyes closed. Her body was filled with suppressed emotions she hadn't known existed until now.

For an instant he gazed down at her as he drew her slowly towards him, then he froze as someone knocked at the door. Her hands tightened against his chest in sudden panic. 'Oh, God. . . We have to talk.' His voice roughened. 'Don't go. Whoever it is, I'll get rid of them.'

She felt dazed, disoriented; her body seemed to be one dull ache of longing. She was aware of the heated colour in her cheeks as, with shaking hands, she struggled to refasten the buttons on her blouse.

She was reaching for her jacket as he went to answer the door and was still struggling into it as the muffled voices came closer.

'Yes, it went very well. I think we should congratulate ourselves, don't. . .?' Helen Crawford's voice trailed away as she glanced beyond Joel, her face contorting briefly as Thea rose stiffly to gather up her bag. 'Oh, I didn't realise you had a visitor,' She said tautly. 'You did say eight. . .' She broke off and Thea's heart gave a painful lurch as she saw the look of annoyance that contorted the other woman's features.

Thea gathered her bag, moving stiffly towards the door. She couldn't think. Her breath seemed to be trapped somewhere in her throat.

'Thea, wait. . .' Joel took her jacket from her, draping it around her shoulders. Brief as it was, the contact was sufficient to reawaken all the feelings she was trying so hard to suppress.

She drew a deep, shuddering breath and broke away. 'Please, I can manage. You'd better go and see to your . . .guest.'

'I'll call you.' His voice roughened as he stood with his hands on her shoulders.

'Goodnight,' she said through stiffened lips. Without looking back, she walked away. Tears burned at the back of her eyelids.

Trust me, he had said, and for a few moments there she had trusted him. But where had it got her? Paul was right, Joel Forrester was an opportunist. He had used her and she had let him, and all the time he must have been thinking about Helen. Shame and humiliation made her tremble as she walked through the darkness. And to think she had been on the verge of weakening. Well, thank God, she had come to her senses in time. She owed Helen Crawford a vote of thanks for that at least.

So why, some small inner voice rose to torment her, did she feel so cheated?

CHAPTER NINE

Two days later, a pale sun broke through the early morning mist as Thea headed along the island's coast road before turning inland and finally bumping her way along a farmyard track.

Bringing the vehicle to a halt, she dragged her wellingtons from the Land Rover, slipping her feet into them before making her way precariously across the yard towards the stone-built house. The door was opened by a tall, blonde-haired girl just as she reached it.

'Morning, Ros. Jim rang the practice. I gather there's a bit of a problem?'

'Hi, nice to see you. Yes, that's right.' Drying her hands on a tea-towel, Ros Francis fielded a toddler about to make his escape through the open door. 'No, you don't, young man.' Lifting the lively two-year-old on to her hip, she gestured towards a row of outbuildings. 'Jim's over there somewhere. If you can hang on a second I'll come with you.' A phone rang somewhere in the distance. 'Damn! No peace for the wicked.'

'Don't worry.' Thea grinned. 'I can find my own way. Anyway, it looks as if you've got your hands pretty full as it is.'

The harassed young woman's face relaxed into a smile. 'You can say that again. I seem to be getting nowhere fast this morning, and I dare say the farmhands will be in in about ten minutes, wanting their breakfast.'

Lucky farmhands, Thea thought, as the smell of frying bacon followed her across the yard. Her own breakfast had been a hastily grabbed cup of coffee and now she was beginning to regret it as her stomach gave a loud rumble.

A raw wind blew in across the fields and she gasped with relief as she made her way into the largest of the buildings.

Jim Francis had set up his pig-breeding unit five years ago and was doing very nicely. Young and enthusiastic, he had inherited a run-down mixed farm, and had taken a decision to specialise in pigs, and Thea admired the determination with which he had gone about it.

Depressingly, she still came across a few farmers who housed their animals in yards, at worst in the open air, or in makeshift buildings, but here the units had been purpose-built and it was a pleasure to walk into the clean, warm, draught-free building, despite the noise of fifty squealing piglets.

Jim was in one of the pens with his pigman, where they were filling the rows of troughs with feed. Tall, stockily built, always smiling, Jim turned at her approach.

'You got here fast.'

'You were first on the list. Morning, Sam,' she greeted the other man. 'Anyway, I know you don't call me out unless you've got a real problem.'

'Hopefully it's nothing too serious.' Jim wiped his hands on his overalls as he climbed out of the pen. 'One of the new litters isn't looking too good. I can't quite put my finger on the problem so I thought it best to get you out to take a look.'

'You did the right thing. Better safe than sorry. Are they in the suckling pens?'

'No, I kept them separate, at least until we know what the problem is. They're over here.'

One hand dug deep in the pocket of her jacket, Thea followed him through to the area kept for farrowing sows. 'How old is the litter?'

'About ten days. They're in here.' Jim led the way into the pen. 'We've kept the sow in a farrowing crate to protect the piglets.'

'Oh, yes, I see what you mean.' Frowning, Thea dropped her bag and, lifting each of the protesting piglets in turn, made a thorough inspection. 'You haven't noticed any coughing?' She glanced up.

Jim shook his head. 'No. You're thinking of pneumonia?'

'Well, it's always a possibility.' Thea put the last of the piglets down and straightened up. 'It can be passed from the sow to the litter, though I must say she looks healthy enough. Let's just take her temperature. Problems with the litter can often start with the sow. Mm — forty degrees.' She withdrew the thermometer. 'Well, that seems normal enough. So, let's see what we've got.' She studied the piglets. 'I see what you mean about them not thriving.' The skin was pale, their ears yellowy. 'Have you noticed any diarrhoea?'

'Well, now that you mention it, yes.'

'What colour?'

He pulled a face. 'Grey mostly.'

Thea nodded. 'This little chap's breathing is not so good either, and that one's looking decidedly frail.' She straightened up again. 'It's just as well you called me, otherwise you'd probably end up losing the whole litter and any future ones.'

'Any idea what's causing it?'

'Actually it's a straightforward case of anaemia.' Thea smiled. 'It's caused by a deficiency of iron in the sow's blood. That in turn causes a shortage of iron in her milk which affects the litter.'

Jim Francis's face relaxed. 'So you can do something about it?'

'I can give them all an iron preparation. It can be administered either through injection or dosing. I think we'll go for the injection, just to be sure. We'd better see to Mum as well, while I'm here, then, hopefully, the problem will be solved.' She was already opening her bag and reaching for a syringe.

'I'm glad I called you. How about a cup of tea and some breakfast?' he said as she administered the final injection.

Thea sighed regretfully and felt her stomach gurgle

in complaint. 'I'd love to, but I've got another call to make so I'd better get on. Thanks for the offer though, and give my regards to Ros. She was up to her eyes so I didn't stop to chat.'

He grinned as he escorted her across the yard to the Land Rover. 'The little un's a real live-wire. By the way, any news about old Bill Parker? We were at the fête when he was whisked off to hospital.'

Dropping her bag on to the seat, Thea climbed in behind the wheel. 'I rang the hospital this morning, as a matter of fact. They won't say too much, obviously, but I gather he's making progress.'

'Thanks to you and Dr Forrester.'

'I'm afraid I didn't do much.'

'Oh, I don't know, it looked like a pretty good effort all round to me.' Jim Francis grinned and Thea felt the colour rise faintly to her cheeks. 'It's nice to have a bit of fresh blood in the community. Livens things up a bit.'

It certainly did that, Thea thought, as she bowled back along the narrow lanes a couple of hours later.

The waiting-room was empty when finally she got back to the practice and walked through to Reception.

'Hi.' Karen greeted her arrival with a smile. 'Had a busy morning?'

'You could say.' Thea dumped her bag to chafe her hands. 'It was all going quite nicely until I got to the Mortimer place.'

'Oh, no. What happened?'

'Two of his calves are down with scours. I'm only surprised it hasn't happened long before this. It's all down to bad stock management. He keeps those animals in cold, wet, stinking conditions, then has the nerve to be surprised when they don't thrive.' Thea ran an agitated hand through her hair. 'That man should have retired years ago.'

Karen gave a short laugh. 'Try telling Walt Mortimer that.'

'I did,' Thea gave a wry, answering smile, 'and a fat lot of good it did me.'

'Could you do anything to help?'

'Apart from delivering a lecture, which I know will go totally unheeded, oh, yes, I handed out son.e drugs. But I won't be too surprised to get another call in the not too distant future. Thank heavens farmers like Walt Mortimer are a rarity these days.'

Karen smiled. 'Coffee?'

'Wonderful. You're a lifesaver. Has Andrew left yet?'

'Mm, about fifteen minutes ago. He muttered something about last-minute shopping, forgotten the wine or something, and headed out at a rate of knots. I gather you're going to the party tonight. I got an invite but I had something else already lined up, more's the pity.'

Thea nodded, gratefully accepting a mug of steaming coffee. 'I'm quite looking forward to it. I haven't seen Joanne and the boys for ages. Any messages for me, by the way?'

Karen hunted for her notepad. 'Er. . .yes. Tom Craddock rang to say the formalin and copper sulphate did the trick. The foot rot has cleared.'

'Oh, good.'

'And. . .' Karen flipped the page, 'Uh, yes, Dr Forrester rang.'

Thea's breath snagged in her chest. Graphic images of Joel and Helen Crawford had haunted her over the last couple of days. She had tried to shut them out but they had remained, painfully to taunt her until, in the end, she had told herself she didn't care. She wouldn't let herself care. There was no future in it. 'Any message?'

'No, except to say perhaps you could call him at the surgery?'

Damn! 'Now?' Thea stared with agonised concentration at her watch.

'He said he'll be there until midday.'

'In that case I suppose I'd better do it now. Thanks,

Karen.' Stifling a sigh, Thea made her way to the office,
reached for the phone and dialled the number. It was
answered almost immediately, as if the person at the
other end had been waiting for it to ring.

'Yes?'

'Joel, it's Thea.'

'I know who it is.'

'You left a message asking me to call.'

There was a moment's silence. 'I don't think I
thanked you properly for what you did the other day.'

'Your mind was obviously on other, more important
things.' She kept the response purposely light, almost
flippant. She had promised herself she would stay calm,
not get emotional. She couldn't even see him yet he
still managed to affect her. 'It isn't necessary,' she said.
'Was that all, only I'm rather busy. . .?'

'Thea, wait!'

She swallowed hard. It was ridiculous. All it took
was the sound of his voice to bring the memories
rushing back.

'I meant what I said, Thea. We have to talk.'

'There's nothing to say.' She was battling against a
feeling of panic. Out of sight might not be out of mind
in Joel Forrester's case, but it was certainly safer.

'You're crazy, you know that?' he murmured softly.
'You're a walking disaster area. Anyone in his right
senses would run a mile, but maybe that's the trouble.
When I'm around you, common sense seems to fly out
of the window.'

She leaned her head against the door and closed her
eyes. Don't do this to me, she begged silently.

'We have to meet, Thea, and talk.' The words were
a whisper in her ear. She could imagine his mouth,
sensuous, dangerous. . .

She jerked upright.

'Scared, Thea?' he breathed.

It was too close to the truth for comfort. She
struggled against the feeling of desire that washed over

her. 'I'm out tonight.' She wished the ground would open up even as she said it.

'As it happens, so am I.'

With the lovely Helen, no doubt. Common sense returned like a life-saving deluge of cold water, bringing her back to earth. 'I really do have work to do. Give my regards to Miss Crawford, by the way.'

She didn't wait to hear what effect her parting shot had. The growl in his throat was sufficient to make her slam down the phone, and she laughed as she walked out to her car.

Paul gazed with undisguised admiration as she emerged from the bedroom, performing a twirl for his benefit. 'I didn't know what to wear so I went out and bought this.' She came to a halt, frowning anxiously. 'You don't think it's a bit over-the-top for an anniversary party, do you?'

'I think it's absolutely perfect.' Taking her in his arms, Paul kissed her and she returned the gesture passively. She wasn't going to allow her evening to be ruined by Joel Forrester. All the same, she couldn't help wondering how he would have reacted to the burgundy velvet dress which hugged her waist and hips. Knee-length, with a scooped neckline and a matching jacket, it had made her fall in love with it the moment she had seen it in the boutique. Now, suddenly, she wasn't so sure.

It certainly wasn't the kind of dress she would normally have chosen. Maybe she was rebelling, subconsciously, against the practical, everyday wear of jeans and sweaters, and then came an uncomfortable awareness that, in a way, it had almost been for his benefit. A defiant gesture which would serve no useful purpose at all, she reminded herself crossly, because he wouldn't be there to see it.

She was unaware that she sighed involuntarily until Paul held her in his arms and kissed her again.

'You look gorgeous. So gorgeous in fact that I wish

we didn't have to go to this damn party tonight,' he
drawled softly. 'I'd much rather have you to myself.'

She returned his kiss, smiling. 'We have to go.'

Taking her jacket from her, he draped it over her
shoulders, his hands lingering as he brushed a kiss
against her cheek. 'I want you to know that if I seemed
to push you the other day, it's only because I want
things settled between us. I do love you, you know
that?'

'Yes, of course I do.' Thea returned his kiss. The
thought that he was going to be beside her gave her a
comforting feeling, so that she relaxed. As if sensing a
change in her, Paul's kiss became more demanding. For
a moment she stood motionless, a feeling of vague
panic tightening her throat. Why was it so difficult to
make a decision?

She managed to evade him lightly as he pulled her
towards him again. 'Hadn't we better go? We're due at
Andrew and Joanne's in half an hour.'

He released her with obvious reluctance. 'I suppose
you're right. Damn it, why do we have to go out?'

'Because we promised,' she laughed gently. And
besides, she needed some space to try to think, to get
her confused thoughts into some sort of order.

'I'm so glad you could come.' Joanne greeted their
arrival with obvious pleasure. A tall, dark-haired
woman of about thirty-five, she had attractive looks
which were emphasised by the soft Angora figure-
hugging cowl-necked dress she was wearing. She raised
her voice above the sound of music. 'I know it's
ridiculous but I feel so nervous,' she confided with a
smile. 'I don't know why I let myself in for this sort of
thing.'

'It's not every day you celebrate ten happy years of
marriage.' Thea smiled, handing her a bouquet of
flowers.

'Oh, aren't they gorgeous?' Joanne inhaled their
fragrance. 'Look, come through and have a drink and
meet people.' She led the way into the lounge. 'I think

you know everyone. I purposely kept it to just a few close friends. Ben and Alice Grant, our neighbours and friends from way back, when Andrew was still struggling to get through veterinary college.'

'It sounds like quite a party.' As she slipped off her jacket, Thea heard voices through the open door. The shock of seeing Joel left her momentarily immobilised and she groaned inwardly. With a pang she noticed how attractive he looked in the dark lounge suit.

He was standing with a glass in his hand beside Helen Crawford, who looked staggeringly attractive in a dress which, Thea was certain, hadn't been bought locally.

For a moment, as she stood frozen in the doorway, his gaze rose and she took an involuntary step backwards, then Andrew was making them welcome, inviting them in and offering them drinks.

'I hardly need to introduce you to Joel, and Helen, Helen Crawford, our local district nurse,' Joanne made the introductions, blissfully unaware of any tension. 'I gather you've already met.'

Beside her, Thea was aware of Paul stiffening. 'Forrester.'

Joel's dark head moved in brief acknowledgement before his glittering gaze moved with slow deliberation to Thea. A tremor of desire ran through her as his dark eyes travelled over her. Her body responded as though he had touched her, sending a wave of heat rushing through her. She closed her eyes to shut him out.

'Everything's under control in the kitchen,' Joanne said. 'We've time for an aperitif. What will it be?'

'Sherry please. Dry. I'll just. . .freshen up first, if you don't mind?' Thea looked at Paul. 'You go ahead. I'll join you in a minute.'

She fled to the bathroom, her legs shaking, and leaned for a moment against the door. It simply hadn't occurred to her that Joel would be here, yet, when she thought about it, she realised that she shouldn't have been surprised since both men were friends, both involved in the local community.

She groaned softly. This was ridiculous. Everything was getting out of hand. There was a whole evening to get through. Somehow she was going to have to smile and be polite.

They were all talking animatedly as she returned to the lounge. Paul and Alice Grant were engaged in deep conversation. Joanne was laughing with Neil and Fay Thomas, local shopkeepers. Andrew was showing some holiday snaps to Helen, leaving Joel to bring her glass of sherry. She took it, careful to avoid any physical contact and said, stiffly, 'When you said you were going to be out tonight I didn't realise you meant here.'

One dark eyebrow rose. 'Would it have made any difference? I imagine we're both here because Andrew and Joanne are friends, not for any ulterior motive.' His lips quirked. 'I'm not about to leap on you, Thea, no matter how strong the motivation. I happen to believe there's a time and place for all things.'

No, of course he wasn't, not with the lovely Helen present. Even so, she felt the surge of hot colour in her cheeks.

Paul's gaze rose above Alice Grant's shoulder and Thea noticed that his face briefly lost its animated look, to be replaced by one of faint displeasure, but, if he noticed, there was no sign of it on Joel's face as he said softly, 'We will talk, Thea.'

It was with relief that she heard Joanne's announcement that they could eat. Her heart performed a crazy little dance as Joel's hand came down on her arm. It faded to a dull thump as Paul came towards her and she found herself relinquished almost too quickly into his care. For the rest of the evening, she sat opposite Joel, who seemed to direct the conversation and easy laughter so that no one noticed that she had hardly touched the salmon terrine.

'So, how have you settled in?' Alice directed the question to Joel as she helped herself to vegetables. 'I gather you've been abroad. Lucky you.'

Joel smiled. 'For the past three years, yes.'

'It can't be easy settling into a small community.'

'Oh, I don't know.' Paul drained his wine glass in one swallow. 'Some people might quite enjoy being a big fish in a small pond, especially when the ground-work has already been done, so to speak.'

Thea was conscious of the sudden silence around the table. Swallowing hard, she managed to say lightly, 'Bob was certainly popular. I think we're enormously lucky to have someone to fill his place. . .'

'We should be so lucky.' Paul's lips twisted as he frowned at his empty glass. 'I've heard it's a pretty good life out in Canada. In fact, we've been thinking we might give it a try, isn't that right, Thea? What do you think, Forrester? Give us an expert's opinion.'

Joel's blue eyes narrowed briefly. 'It's certainly a land of opportunity, for those prepared to work.'

'Oh, I'm not afraid of hard work, provided the rewards are there, of course. In fact — ' Paul suddenly reached out to clasp Thea's hand, his thumb brushing against her fingers ' — we've been giving it a lot of serious thought, haven't we, darling?'

Looking at him, sitting so taut and hunched over the table, she had to swallow hard to get rid of the lump in her throat as she said quietly, 'It's a big decision. Not something to be decided in a hurry.'

Joanne, at the other end of the table, was engrossed in conversation with Fay Thomas. She giggled as her glass was refilled. At least someone was having a good time, Thea thought.

Dessert was served in frost-rimmed glasses and she toyed with the delicate syllabub, watching unhappily as Paul reached for the bottle, refilling his glass. Maybe tiredness was making him irritable.

She looked up to find Joel watching her, his expression unreadable. His mouth tightened. She sensed that he was angry without quite knowing why, yet when he spoke his voice remained even.

'As you say, it rather depends on what you want out of life, on a personal as well as a professional level.'

'Of course, some people find it difficult to put down roots anywhere, like to keep moving on.' Paul thrust his empty glass away impatiently.

It was almost a relief when they adjourned for coffee and Thea couldn't help noticing that Joel didn't seem to mind in the least the proprietorial way in which Helen Crawford slipped her arm through his, as if she was staking her claim. And why not? she thought dully; after all, she has the right.

'Go through to the lounge,' Andrew directed. 'I'll be with you in a minute. Joel, there's a rather nice bottle of port somewhere. Would you look in the cupboard in the library?'

'I'd better just check on the boys,' Joanne excused herself as they moved into the sitting-room, to find it suffused by the glow from the fire and a lamp.

Ben and Alice Grant had made their excuses and left. 'Baby-sitters, you know how it is, and one of the children has a bit of a temperature.' Neil and Fay Thomas followed shortly afterwards.

A tray of freshly made coffee had been left on one of the small tables. Thea moved purposefully towards it, wondering how long it would be before they could reasonably make their own excuses to leave. The meal had been lovely and cooked to perfection, but it had all tasted like chaff in her mouth.

'I'll pour. Cream?'

'Leave it,' Paul insisted, drawing her into his arms. 'God, I thought we were never going to be alone.'

She cast an anxious glance at the door. 'Someone might come in.'

'To hell with them.' His mouth tightened sullenly. 'It's bad enough having to listen to that supercilious bastard all day. I don't have to pretend to be sociable in my own time.' He prised the coffee-pot from her hands, putting it on the tray. 'Anyway, so what if they do? We're supposed to be a couple.'

Thea winced at the slight emphasis he placed on the

word. 'Was it necessary to make your feelings quite so obvious?'

'I don't know why it happens,' he said gruffly. 'It seems I only have to be around Forrester for the sparks to start flying. I know it's crazy.' He drew her closer, brushing a hand against her cheek. She could smell the wine on his breath. 'I suppose the truth is that I'm jealous.'

'Jealous!' She laughed slightly, feeling the colour burn into her cheeks.

'It must be the way he looks at you.' He raised her face between his hands and kissed her. 'I know I said I didn't want to pressure you, but the waiting is driving me mad. I need to know, Thea. I want my life settled.'

She brushed a strand of hair from her eyes. 'Oh, Paul, I know I said I would think about it but you promised to give me time. . .'

'How much time does it take?' Suddenly he seemed angry. He released her abruptly, moving steadily to the decanter which stood on the bureau. 'Damn the coffee. I need a proper drink.'

She watched as he poured a generous measure, then, as much to dissuade him tactfully not to drink any more, as because she was suddenly eager to get away, she said gently, 'Perhaps we should leave? You're right, if I need to do some serious thinking I'll do it better when I can have peace and quiet.'

Paul stared moodily into his glass, discarded it and came to put his hands on her shoulders. 'Just say yes, Thea. That's all it takes.'

She felt her heart contract painfully, as if she were being dragged into something deeper than she wanted to go, but it made no sense. It's because I'm tired, she told herself, surrendering her mouth to his and feeling a vague stirring of her emotions. She was very fond of Paul; she enjoyed being with him. But were they the kind of qualities which made for a long and happy marriage? a tiny inner voice rose to torment her.

Perhaps if she closed her eyes and pretended it was

Joel. . . Her mouth trembled hungrily. She felt Paul's
momentary hesitation before he responded more
fiercely.

'Say you'll come with me, Thea. Say you'll marry
me.'

The bubble burst. She wanted to say it but the words
wouldn't come, because—suddenly the truth hit her—
she didn't love Paul.

Her eyes flew open in a moment of panic and she
became instantly aware of the figure standing in the
doorway, the mockery in his eyes turning to contempt
as he took in her flushed cheeks and the glazed look in
her eyes.

She struggled to free herself from Paul's embrace,
feeling sick and conscious only of Joel's stony
expression. It was all too obvious he had drawn his own
conclusions.

'Forgive me.' His voice was icy. 'I seem to have
intruded at the wrong moment.'

Her mouth opened to explain but it was too late.
Paul was thrusting her bag into her hands then his hand
was under her elbow and he was steering her towards
the door.

'Don't worry about it.' His voice slurred slightly. 'We
were just about to leave. Thea isn't feeling well, are
you, darling?'

She was vaguely aware of saying her goodbyes before
she found herself being ushered, protesting, into the
chilly darkness.

'Paul, please. . .'

It had begun to rain. She shivered, following him
blindly to the car, waiting as he fumbled for his keys.
He dropped them and for the first time it hit her that
he was drunk.

'Perhaps you'd better let me drive.'

'I'm not drunk, if that's what you think.'

'I hope you're not thinking of driving, Prescott?' She
heard Joel's voice rasp icily from somewhere in the
darkness. 'If so, I wouldn't recommend it.'

'What the. . .?' Paul dropped the keys again and bent to fumble for them. 'I don't know what the hell you're insinuating, Forrester. . . Get in the car, Thea.'

'I'm not insinuating anything. It's pretty obvious.' Thea gasped as Joel's hand came down firmly on her arm. 'I'll take you home.'

'There's no need,' she gulped hard on a feeling of relief. 'I can walk.' The steely grip merely tightened.

'Put your own life at risk if you choose, Prescott. But at least have the decency not to take anyone else with you.'

'Really, I think I'd rather walk.'

'I'm not in the mood for arguments, Thea.' Taking her arm, Joel marched her, struggling to his own car and thrust her effortlessly into the passenger seat. It was only as she sank into the soft leather that she realised her head was aching and, for once, she felt too weary to argue.

'You have no right to interfere,' Paul blustered. 'Thea. . .?'

For some reason she found herself unable to respond to his appeal.

'I suggest you take a long walk,' Joel grated. 'It may help to sober you up.' He started up the engine and wound down his window. 'As for emergency cover, I'll take over. I hardly think you're in any fit state.'

Without being aware of it, Thea's sickened gaze flew to Paul. She must have misunderstood. Surely he couldn't have been on call?

She didn't need to ask the question aloud. The answer was written guiltily all over his face and she put her head back, closing her eyes. Even worse, she heard him already making excuses and she couldn't bear to see him blustering and red-faced.

Joel didn't even glance in her direction as he swung the car into the road and said curtly, 'You crazy little idiot. Didn't you realise he was drunk? You're damn lucky I came along when I did.'

She ground her teeth furiously. He was doing it

again, taking charge of her life without as much as a by-your-leave. 'I was perfectly all right. You needn't have interfered.' She gave him a truculent stare and a faint smile tugged at the corners of his sensuous mouth.

'You mean I should simply have stood by and let you get killed?'

In the semi-darkness she saw him look at her now and felt the colour flare in her cheeks. Her voice wavered lamely, 'I don't see how Paul could have been drunk. He only had two glasses of wine and a brandy.'

'That's more than enough. Besides, that's only what you saw. How many did he have before he arrived?'

The question stung as it seemed to reinforce her own nagging doubts. 'I could still have managed to find my own way home. Besides,' she couldn't resist, 'won't Helen be rather annoyed to find herself deserted? I don't imagine this is quite what she had in mind.'

'Don't let it bother you,' he said evenly. 'Helen is a free agent. I'm sure she's also resourceful enough to find her own way home.'

Thea choked back a cry of disbelief. How could he be so casual? Obviously it came with years of practice, she told herself, turning to stare blindly out of the window. He was an arrogant, unsympathetic beast, and she hated him.

She sat in silence for the remainder of the journey, feeding a cloud of resentment until the car purred to a halt outside her cottage.

She reached for the door-handle as Joel released his seat belt, but if she had hoped to be able to make her escape she felt a surge of panic as he got out to stand beside her.

'Thanks for the lift,' she said weakly. 'I'm rather tired, so I'll say goodnight.'

'I'm not in the habit of leaving a woman standing on the doorstep, Thea. In any case, I thought it might be a good opportunity to see Wellie.'

Swallowing down her annoyance, she allowed him to

take the keys from her nerveless grasp and unlock the door. Jess ambled sleepily from the kitchen.

'Fine watchdog you are,' Thea dropped her bag on to the table, bending to fondle the dog's ears, then laughed involuntarily as Wellie, tail thumping, abandoned his bed to throw himself at Joel's knees.

He bent to make a fuss of the Labrador. 'Hello, old fellow. Glad to see me, are you? I've missed you too.' He glanced up. 'He looks marvellous.'

'He's not completely out of the woods yet, and you have to remember, his age is against him. On the other hand, he's not in any pain and he seems happy.' She smiled slightly. 'In fact I see no reason why you can't take him home. I'll make some coffee.'

Swallowing on the sudden tightness in her throat, she headed for the kitchen. When she emerged, minutes later, carrying the tray into the sitting-room, Joel was sitting in an armchair, the dog at his feet, looking for all the world as if the pair of them belonged there.

He rose to take the tray from her, placing it on the coffee-table. 'I can scarcely believe the change in him.' He stood watching as Thea poured the coffee. 'A few days ago I wouldn't have given much for his chances.'

'It's all down to good old antibiotics.' Straightening up she held out his cup.

'I think we both know there's more to it than that,' he said softly. 'You've done a marvellous job and I'm grateful, Thea.' His hand brushed against hers, setting her heart thudding from the brief contact. Or had she perhaps drunk a little too much wine? Either way it was a dangerous combination.

'Thea.' His dark, expensively tailored jacket brushed softly against her skin, sending dangerous signals to her brain. 'Don't run away from me.' His voice was uneven as he drew her towards him, his hand against the small of her back, bringing the softness of her curves against his rugged masculinity.

She looked at him and felt a sensation of pure excitement run through her. She could deny it aloud as much as she liked, but the sheer sensuality, the animal magnetism of him sent a wave of desire rushing like a flame through her body.

'Joel, I. . .'

He frowned, then, slowly, his expression changed to one of something like wonderment. 'Thea?'

'Please, don't,' she protested weakly. This shouldn't be happening. 'I'm too confused.'

'I'd never hurt you, you know that.'

Not intentionally, maybe.

He drew a ragged breath, leaning forward to cup her face in his hands, urgently drawing her closer. 'My God, have you any idea of the effect you have on me?'

How could she not know? She moaned softly as his mouth fastened on hers. The sensation was electric. Thea hesitated only a moment, then her head went back as she gave herself up to the tide of emotions that was sweeping her along. Desire flared out of control. Her hands reached up to draw him closer and, with that vital awareness of her body's needs, another, new sensation penetrated her drugged senses. She was in love with Joel Forrester!

'I want you, Thea,' he murmured as his mouth made teasing advances against her cheek, to the hollow of her throat and back to her lips.

Her body trembled beneath the onslaught. She moaned softly as his hands slid the jacket from her shoulders and finally revealed the exquisite fullness of her breast.

She was incapable of rational thought. Her body swayed closer, restlessly seeking some elusive fulfilment.

Joel stiffened. He released her and she uttered a cry of protest. He swore softly under his breath. Only then did she become aware of it too. Someone was knocking loudly at the door.

'Who on earth. . .?'

'I'll go,' he said, tersely.

Thea's fingers shook as she struggled to restore her

clothes to some sort of order as she listened to the
sound of muffled voices in the hall.

When Joel came back into the room, his expression
was grim and Thea stiffened involuntarily.

'Who was it?'

'There's been an accident,' he said. She felt her
stomach tighten. 'It's Paul. It seems he crashed his car.
He's in hospital.'

CHAPTER TEN

'I HAVE to go to him.'

'I'll take you to the hospital.'

'But you're on call.'

'I have the car phone, Thea. If anyone needs to reach me, they can.'

She was vaguely aware of his hand supporting her as they went in silence to his car.

'Do you know what happened?' she asked hoarsely, as he started the engine. 'How did the police know where to come?'

'Apparently it happened fairly close to Andrew's place. It seems Paul took the bend slightly too fast, skidded on the wet surface and hit a tree. A passing motorist knocked at Andrew's door to ask him to contact the emergency services.'

Thea passed her tongue over her dry lips. 'Is. . .is Paul badly hurt?'

'The police didn't say. He managed to tell them your name, so I think we can reasonably hope it's not too serious.'

She turned her head to stare blankly into the darkness. 'I should have been with him.'

'Why?' His steel-cold eyes narrowed, briefly, as he turned to look at her. 'You're damn lucky to be alive. Prescott shouldn't have been behind the wheel. He was drunk, you know it, I know it, and presumably the police must know it.'

She dashed the back of her hand against her eyes. Even as words rose to her lips in Paul's defence, she bit them back. It was true. She had tried to stop him driving, they both had, but perhaps they hadn't tried hard enough.

She licked her dry lips, all too conscious of Joel's

looming presence beside her as they hurried through the main entrance of the large hospital.

The brightly lit corridors seemed endless as she allowed herself to be led blindly, his hand gripping her elbow, through the busy accident and emergency department where a drunk was complaining loudly as two members of staff attempted to restrain him.

Thea realised she would have wasted valuable time trying to find her way through the labyrinth of departments and corridors alone.

'Wait here.' Joel forced her to sit. 'I'll have a word with Sister.' He disappeared, an imposing, dark-suited figure, returning seconds later with the blue-uniformed figure at his side.

'If you'd like to come into the office for a moment.' Smiling, she led the way. 'I'm Sister Jackson, by the way, Louise Jackson.'

'Can I see Paul?'

'I'm sorry.' She smiled sympathetically, 'but it is rather late. Mr Prescott has just gone up to the ward and we'd rather he rested tonight.'

'How serious is it?' Joel said.

Louise Jackson gave a wry smile. 'He's lucky. We've had far worse in already tonight. Let's see.' She reached for the report book, flipping through the pages. 'He's got a nasty bump on his head but the X-ray showed no fracture. He'll have the mother of all headaches when he wakes up, I dare say. His arm is badly bruised and he has a sprained wrist.' She smiled at Thea. 'He's not going to be running any races for a while, but there's nothing too serious. My advice would be to go home and get some sleep. There's nothing you can do here. The patient will sleep for several hours. By tomorrow he may feel up to chatting.'

'You'll let me know if there's any —— ?'

'I have Dr Forrester's number.' Sister smiled and looked pointedly at her watch. 'And now, if you'll excuse me —— ' she glanced at Joel ' — we have another RTA on its way in and we're short-staffed as usual.'

Thea's head was throbbing as they walked out to the car again. Her hands shook as she fumbled with the door-handle and Joel's hand brushed against hers as he opened it for her.

'He'll be all right.' He climbed into the driver's seat. 'He's damn lucky. Some don't get off so lightly.'

Tears welled up, stinging behind her eyelids. She blinked hard. Joel took his gaze briefly from the road, reached into his pocket and handed her a hanky.

'It's not the end of the world. He's going to be sore and out of action for a while. Just be glad it wasn't a whole lot worse, that no one else was involved.'

'It must be nice to be so cold-blooded,' she snapped. 'You're used to it; it doesn't affect you any longer, does it? You don't see people, you see patients, casualties, victims. Well, just because Paul doesn't react in the same way. . .' She broke off, pressing the back of her hand against her mouth. 'You've never liked Paul, have you? Well, frankly, I'm not surprised he's behaved in the way he has if tonight is an example of the kind of pressure he's been under.'

His voice was clipped. 'Thea,' he said, 'I'll ignore that because you're not thinking rationally.' The car drew to a halt. 'It's been a long day. You should try to get some sleep. I'm sure tomorrow you'll see things more clearly.'

'You certainly won't lose any sleep over it, will you? Your conscience is quite clear.'

His face darkened. 'I'm not responsible for Prescott's stupidity, Thea. What happened was a result of his own actions.'

She climbed out of the car to face him fiercely. 'We were both to blame. You shouldn't have stopped me going with him. If I hadn't let you talk me out of it I might have been able to make him see sense. I should have been more supportive.' Maybe none of this would have happened if she had given Paul the answer he wanted about their future.

Joel's glittering gaze narrowed. 'Were you thinking about Paul when you were in my arms, Thea?'

Hot colour flooded her cheeks. 'Why, you. . .'

His hand caught hers; his fingers brushed against her cheek. 'It's not so nice, facing the truth, is it, Thea? Why don't you admit it? You couldn't have responded to me as you did if you really cared for him.'

'No!'

'Yes, Thea. Be honest with yourself. You don't love him; you never have.' His hand was behind her head, drawing her remorselessly closer as his mouth closed on hers in a kiss which seemed to drive the breath out of her lungs.

There wasn't even time to respond because, as quickly as it had begun, the assault upon her emotions ended, leaving her breathless and, for some reason, bitterly frustrated.

She broke away, breathing hard. 'It isn't true.' She refused to acknowledge the possibility. Paul needed her as Joel never would.

Later, pulling a satin nightshirt over her head, she walked to the bedroom window and stood in the darkness. It was a cool, clear night. Across the field, between the trees, she could just glimpse a small pinpoint of light from the neighbouring cottage.

Tearing herself away, she climbed into bed, pulling the covers over her head. She couldn't think about Joel Forrester. All right, for one crazy moment she had let her guard slip and he had stormed in, taking advantage of a moment of weakness. But she would make very sure it never happened again.

Market day inevitably seemed to bring with it a full surgery, although Thea had never actually worked out the logic behind it.

From the moment the doors opened she was kept busy diagnosing and treating a wide variety of conditions. Her first customer was a budgie with an upset tummy and looking decidedly sorry for itself.

Thea surveyed the ruffled feathers, a sure sign of chilling, the bird's partially closed eyes and the soiling of its rear end by diarrhoea, and her heart sank. Budgies, at best, were notoriously frail creatures but, aware of the child anxiously watching her every move, she forced a smile as she made her examination and said, 'He's certainly not very well, is he? Do you keep him in a cage at home?'

'No, in an aviary, in the garden.'

Thea smiled. 'Oh, so you've got quite a few budgies, then? Are any of the others showing the same signs or is it just this one?' The small boy shook his head and she breathed a small sigh of relief. 'Well, that's good. At least it doesn't sound as if there's an infection of any kind. I think this little chap has probably eaten something that disagreed with him. Too much green food, maybe?'

'I gave them some grass from the roadside. Dad says it's good for them to have green stuff.'

'Yes, well, it is, in small amounts. The problem with greenery from the roadside is that it may not always be very clean,' Thea explained as she gently began to clean the caked droppings from the bird's tail end. 'Grass verges are sometimes sprayed with chemicals, or they can be coated by fumes from passing traffic.' She held the bird gently. 'I've cleaned him up as much as I can. I don't want to handle him too much. He's already quite distressed.'

'But he is going to be all right?'

'I can't promise. He's quite poorly, but I'll give you some antibiotic powder, to put in his drinking water. Just a quarter of a teaspoon at a time. If I were you, I'd keep him in a cage indoors, just for a few days, until he seems better. You could cover the cage with a towel perhaps. That will help him to rest. Keep him warm and, most important of all, when he is better, stick to good quality seed and only give green food sparingly, and when you know that it's clean.' She popped the budgie back into its cardboard container. 'Do you think you can do that?'

He nodded eagerly. 'I'll take care of him. I'll keep him in my bedroom, with my hamster.'

Sandra laughed as he took his leave, carefully clutching the box. 'Another satisfied customer. Let's hope Mum approves of this indoor menagerie. Would you like me to send the next patient in?'

The next hour was taken up advising an owner on the correct diet for an overweight corgi, clipping a terrier's toenails, removing stitches from a cat she had operated on some time ago, following a road accident in which its hip had been broken, and treating a cat with an eye injury.

'He came home like this.' Tall, about forty years old, Mrs Stevens placed the cat basket on the treatment table, leaving Thea to take out the distressed animal. 'We started to get worried when he didn't come home last night. It's not like him. He likes to be warm and he never misses his food,' she explained anxiously. 'Then, this morning, a neighbour brought him home. He found him at the side of the road.'

Thea studied the large, black and white tom cat, stretched out on the table. His eyes were closed. 'It certainly looks as if he may have been hit by a car.'

She examined the cat's head, feeling for signs of injury or bruising and inspected its eyes, gently parting the lids. Using a bright light, she made an inspection and nodded as she completed the examination. 'There's quite a lot of bruising. It's not easy to see because of his fur, but I'd say he's had a blow to the head and there's quite a bit of haemorrhaging, the feline equivalent of black eyes. There's some grit or something in there as well, which is probably why he's not too keen to open his eyes.' She looked at Sandra. 'I'll use a dropper with plain water to try to wash it out.'

Sandra handed her a large wad of cotton-wool from which Thea dripped water into the cat's eyes.

'This should flush out any foreign objects.' Having

completed the procedure, Thea inspected the eyes again. 'Yes, that looks much better.' Again, with the bright light, she did another check. 'I can't see any actual lacerations, which is lucky. So, let's take a look at the rest of the damage, shall we?'

Sandra smiled reassuringly at the anxious pet owner. 'He's probably got quite a nasty headache but he'll soon perk up.'

'What about his paw. There's an awful lot of blood.'

'He's got quite a nasty, deep cut,' Thea frowned as she inspected the wound. 'Apart from that,' she ran her hands gently over the small, furry body, 'I'd say he got off remarkably lightly. His hips. . .yes, they're OK.' Straightening up, she smiled at the woman. 'Look, what I'd like to do is keep him overnight, just so that we can clean him up, pop in a few stitches and put a dressing on that paw. It would give him a bit of a rest, a chance to get over the shock. How do you feel about that?'

'Oh, I'd be so grateful. When will I be able to collect him, only the children will want to know. . .'

'Of course they will.' Thea smiled. 'You can pick him up tomorrow morning. By then he should be looking much brighter. I'll give him an injection of antibiotic so that we can be sure that cut doesn't become infected, and I'll also let you have some pain-killers, just to see him through the next couple of days.'

Mrs Stevens took her leave as Thea washed her hands. 'Right, so what else have we got?'

'Er. . .there's Mrs Reynolds' cat to be spayed, oh, and the setter with the lump.'

Thea nodded, looking at her watch. 'If that's the last of the patients I'll do the stitching now, then I'll do the ops. I shall feel happier once I can confirm that the lump is benign.'

'I hope it is,' Sandra said. 'Old Jack Peters dotes on that dog. It's as old as the hills and probably riddled with fleas but I think he'd give up if anything happened to it. I'll get him prepped, shall I?'

'You're an angel.'

It was lunchtime when Andrew, returning from his calls, stuck his head round the door. 'Hi, how's it going?'

Thea checked the anaesthetised red setter carefully, before looking up and smiling. 'I'm just about finished, thank goodness.' Easing her back she gave a tiny grimace. 'It's been quite a morning. How about you?' She turned to Sandra. 'That's it. Thanks for your help. We'll keep him in the recovery cage and I'll check on him later.' Turning back to Andrew she said, 'I heard you had to go over to St Helier?'

He hauled off his jacket, hanging it on a peg. 'Mm, that's right. A case of streptococcal mastitis. Classic case really.' He hunted in his pocket for his pipe. 'The udders were hot and swollen, clots in the milk, low yield. Thank God for antibiotics.'

'What about the rest of the stock?'

'OK, so far, thank heavens. Ah, is that for me?'

'Thought you might need it.' Sandra placed a large mug of coffee on the table before looking at Thea. 'Is it all right if I pop off now, only I promised I'd collect a few bits of shopping for my mum?'

'Fine,' Thea smiled. 'Talking of which——' she glanced, frowning at the clock '—I suppose I should be making a move. I said I'd visit Paul at the hospital.'

'How is he?'

She pulled a wry face. 'I rang earlier. All they would say was that he is comfortable.'

'Hospital talk.' Andrew chewed at his empty pipe. 'The road must have been pretty wet and that particular bend is notorious. It was a bit of luck Joel decided to pick Wellie up and took you home.'

'Yes, wasn't it?' Thea forced a smile, feeling the heat rise in her cheeks. 'I haven't thanked you yet for a lovely evening, by the way. The food was marvellous. Joanne surpassed herself, as usual. I'll drop her a line to thank her properly.' She reached for her jacket and bag. 'I'd better go. You know what it's like, trying to park.'

'Well, look, I'm going into town myself. I want to drop off some ministry forms and call in at the bank. I can give you a lift if you like?'

'Would you mind?' Thea breathed a sigh of relief. 'I must admit, the thought of battling through the traffic is just too awful.'

'Give me five minutes and I'll be with you.'

The ward was bright with spring flowers and already surprisingly busy as Thea made her way between the rows of beds, searching for Paul. She felt a moment of panic when he was nowhere to be seen and intercepted one of the nurses.

'Excuse me, I'm looking for Dr Prescott but he doesn't seem to be here.'

The tiny, blonde-haired staff nurse frowned. 'Dr Prescott? No, I don't think. . . Oh — ' her attractive features relaxed ' — you mean Paul.' She indicated a door at the end of the ward. 'We put him in one of the side rooms.'

'He's not worse?'

The girl smiled. 'No, he's fine. It's just that we had several admissions after an RTA so we had to do a bit of juggling around. Oh, Nurse — ' she waylaid a passing student ' — take these x-rays back to the department, will you, and tell Dr Patel that Mr Forsythe wants another view of Mr Calder's ankle. Sorry about that,' she smiled ruefully at Thea. 'The consultant was late doing his round. We're still trying to catch up.'

'Can you tell me how Paul is?'

The girl smiled. 'He's nursing a headache. I'm afraid that was inevitable because of the concussion, so he's not too happy. But we've given him some pain-killers.'

'Have you any idea when he'll be allowed out?'

'Ah, well, that isn't up to me, but barring any problems I should think he'll probably be able to go tomorrow. Once the registrar gives the all-clear. Yes, Nurse,' she acknowledged the student nurse waving a telephone in her direction. 'I'm on my way. Sorry about this. Visiting time is supposed to be a quiet period. It never works that way for the staff.'

Her attractively slim figure moved towards the nursing station, leaving Thea to make her way to the small side room.

Paul was lying with his eyes closed, his head resting against the pillows when she quietly pushed the door open. She looked at him, his face pale, the darkening bruise shadowing his forehead. It was odd to find herself looking at him as if expecting something to have changed, but nothing had.

She said softly, 'Hello, Paul.'

He opened his eyes, blinked hard and grinned sheepishly. 'Hi. I was afraid maybe you wouldn't be talking to me ever again. I was even toying with the idea of sending out a mayday.'

For some reason she found herself failing to respond to his attempt at humour. Looking at him, to see him grin now, it was almost as if the accident had never happened. There wasn't even a hint of remorse that, had Joel not come along to prevent it, she might so easily have been a victim too, and the thought made her speak more sharply than she had intended.

'At least you're still in one piece.' She dropped the magazines she had brought with her on to the locker. 'I thought you might like to have these, although I suppose, if you have a headache, you won't feel much like reading. You'll have to let me know if there's anything. . .'

Paul caught hold of her arm, drawing her to a halt as she made to sit in the chair. 'Thea, I want you to know, I feel rotten about what happened. I behaved like a bloody idiot.' He brushed a hand across his eyes. 'I don't know what happened. I can vaguely remember saying a lot of stupid things. . .'

She felt like saying that she knew very well, that he had had too much to drink and behaved childishly, but it seemed pointless and, judging from his expression, he was more than paying for it.

She moved restlessly beneath the pressure of his restraining hand and sat on the bed. 'Why don't we just try to forget it? I can't stay long. . .'

'It's not so easy.' His hand tightened over hers. 'I realise we can't talk here, now, Thea. But later. There are things we have to get straight. Will you see me when I get out of here.'

'Yes, of course, you know I will, Paul.'

'That's not what I meant.' He sat up, wincing as he did so. 'I still want you to come away with me, Thea. I know I've been a damn fool, but surely what we have together is too good to throw away?'

She stared at him, wondering what exactly it was that she and Paul had, or ever did have. She had always been content simply to go along with things, to enjoy their friendship, until now. Maybe somehow, some-where along the way, they had begun to drift apart without her even being aware of it. Or maybe she hadn't wanted to be aware. The thought brought the colour to her cheeks.

She cut him off, knowing that she was being deliber-ately ruthless. 'I know I promised, Paul, but I really haven't had a chance to think about it.'

'But you will, won't you?' he pleaded. 'Look, I won't rush you. Just say that what's happened won't make a difference. I'll call you, as soon as I get out of here. We'll talk.'

'Yes, do that.' In an agitated movement she rose to her feet. 'I really do have to go.' Looking at her watch, she stepped back, gasping as she made contact with a solid male figure.

The strong pair of arms in whose grasp she was held, tightened slowly as an all too familiar voice said calmly, 'I had a feeling I might find you here.'

'You!' Her gaze locked with the deep blue eyes which regarded her with a hint of amused arrogance. She stiffened, gritting her teeth as the hot colour scorched into her cheeks. Her heart was behaving ridiculously too as she tore herself from his grasp. 'As a matter of fact I was just leaving.'

'Don't rush away on my account.'

She shot him a look. 'What are you doing here anyway?'

'I'm a doctor.' Blue eyes glittered. 'It's my job to visit patients, remember? As a matter of fact, I had to visit a new mum in the community maternity unit and thought I'd kill two birds with one stone, so to speak, by popping in to see how our own patient is progressing.' He looked at Paul. 'How's the head?'

'Thumping, as a matter of fact,' Paul replied, irritably.

'Yes, well, I imagine it would. Hangovers tend to have that effect.' Joel's gaze swept contemptuously over Paul, who was now a deathly white. 'Perhaps you should thank your lucky stars that no one else was hurt. At least it needn't go any further.'

Thea licked her dry lips. 'You mean. . .the police won't be taking any further action?'

He shrugged. 'As I said, no one else was injured. The road was wet at the time.' The blue gaze narrowed as he looked at her. 'We certainly don't need the kind of publicity that would be aroused if it got around that one of our doctors is a drunk driver. As far as I'm concerned, the less said, the better.' He glanced at the chart at the end of Paul's bed. 'I imagine you'll be up and around within twenty-four hours, provided you behave.'

'I don't exactly have much choice, do I?'

'Not much,' Joel said, stonily. 'In the meantime, I'll cover the surgeries and emergency calls. We'll talk, once you're back in circulation, and see where we go from here.'

Paul looked as if he had been pole-axed. Thea's hand stole to her throat. Too many conflicting emotions seemed to be whirling around inside her head. She was glad he hadn't been badly hurt. The fact that he had brought it upon himself scarcely seemed relevant, but it didn't blind her either to the fact that she was seeing a whole new side of him which she hadn't been aware of before, and she didn't much like what she was seeing.

She cleared her throat. 'I have to go.'

'Thea?' Paul uttered plaintively.

She forced a smile, kissing him lightly on the cheek. 'I really must go. The bus leaves in ten minutes. I'll see you tomorrow.'

It was almost a relief to hear the bell signalling an end to visiting time as she hurried down the ward. She had reached the swing doors when a strong male hand pushed them open.

'I'll give you a lift,' Joel told her.

She swallowed hard. 'Thanks for the offer, but there's no need. The bus will be along in a minute.' Anything, rather than having to share the close proximity of a car with him, she thought.

His eyes took on a steely quality as he walked beside her, across to where he had parked the car. 'Don't push your luck, Thea.' He held the door open. 'It's been a long day so far. Besides which, I think you'll find the bus has already left and it's a long walk home.'

Dismayed, she followed his gaze just in time to see the bus disappearing into the distance. She closed her eyes on a feeble and totally unsuccessful attempt to shut him out of her thoughts. Being near him only seemed to compound the sense of guilt that was beginning to torment her. Her nerves seemed to have become an emotional battlefield, with the enemy on both sides and nowhere to run.

Almost before she knew it, she was installed in the car and Joel was climbing in beside her. He made a few perfunctory remarks, but, apart from that, drove in silence. It was a relief. It gave her a chance to stare out of the window, to try and put her thoughts in order. Except that it didn't seem to work somehow. Her feelings for Joel Forrester were not something that could be neatly indexed and filed away for later, more

was the pity. She wasn't aware that she had sighed until
his gaze drifted briefly from the road to her face.

'A penny for them.'

She blinked hard. Her thoughts weren't for sale — at
any price! 'Actually I was thinking about Maggie
Pemberton.' The lie came with disconcerting ease.

He manoeuvred the car deftly into the stream of
early afternoon traffic before glancing in her direction
again. 'As a matter of fact, I was going to tell you: she
was on my visiting list as well, today. She's doing fine.
In fact, she's making such good progress, she may be
allowed home in a couple of days.'

'Oh, that's marvellous news. But. . .will she be able
to cope?'

'Not alone, obviously.' His dark brows drew
together. 'We shall have to get social services involved,
providing back-up. There's always a danger that the
elderly can become institutionalised if they are out of
their own environment for too long. Personally, I think
that, if they can be offered the right support, they're
better off at home.'

'Even so, it won't be easy.'

'I realise that.' He gave a slight smile. 'Maggie's an
elderly lady, an independent, elderly lady maybe, but I
think even she will admit that the time has come when
she has to think about accepting some help.'

In spite of herself, Thea found herself laughing.
'Admitting it is one thing, getting Maggie to accept it is
quite another.'

A smile tugged at his mouth. 'I shall have to bring all
my powers of persuasion to bear.'

And heaven help Maggie, Thea thought. She won't
know what's hit her. She dragged her thoughts away,
realising, with a sudden start, that the car had come to
a halt at a small, thatch-roofed pub, its garden running
to the edge of a river. With a touch of apprehension
she stared out of the window. 'Why have we stopped?'

'Relax.' Joel's expression hardened. 'I don't know
about you, but personally I find I function better if I

manage to fit in a meal every now and then. I need to eat.'

He held the door and Thea reluctantly climbed out. 'Isn't it a little late for lunch?'

'This place is open all day. It caters for tourists.' His hand was firm beneath her elbow as he led the way into the oak-beamed interior. 'I've been here before. The food's good.'

With the lovely Helen, no doubt! She felt her cheeks redden as his eyebrows rose quizzically.

'Hungry?'

If it hadn't been for the fact that her stomach chose that precise moment to rumble loudly, she might have denied it. As it was, having discovered her appetite and guessing that, whatever her decision, he intended to eat anyway, why cut her nose off to spite her face?

She ate ravenously and when finally she replaced her knife and fork, having demolished the last flake of delicate puff pastry, the last melting mouthful of home-made steak and kidney pie, she found it disconcerting to look up and see him watching her, a glint of amusement darkening his eyes.

'I like to see someone with a healthy appetite.'

She blushed, guiltily, as she realised he had opted for a salad. 'Bang goes the diet again.'

'Don't apologise for enjoying something, Thea, and there's absolutely nothing wrong with your figure. Would you like coffee?'

'Yes, please.' She wished she could ignore the tiny *frisson* of pleasure that ran through her at the genuine note of admiration in his voice.

'We'll take it outside. There are some tables by the river.'

They emerged, blinking, into the sunlight after the cool interior.

'Come and look at the river. We might see some trout.'

Thea stood still, absorbing the beauty of the water lapping against the stones. 'It's lovely here,' she murmured. 'So clean and fresh, unspoiled. How did you know it was here? It must be way off the beaten track.'

'I found it quite by chance one day. Look,' Joel said softly, 'there's a kingfisher.'

Lowering her voice, she followed the direction of his pointing finger. 'Where? I don't see it?'

'Over there on that lower branch overhanging the water.' His hand settled on her waist.

Turning her head she felt the warmth of his breath on her cheek as she looked into his eyes instead, and knew a feeling of total confusion.

She heard him draw a breath and found herself battling to keep her own breathing even. 'I. . .don't think this is a good idea.'

He made no attempt to let her go, his tautly muscled body so close that she could feel the thud of his heart. He turned her slowly to face him and, before she knew what he was doing, he bent his head, brushing his lips lightly against her mouth.

The effect was devastating and she responded almost involuntarily.

'Thea, oh, Thea.' He spoke softly and she opened her eyes to find his deep blue gaze on her.

It was unfair, she thought, as he kissed her again. She felt as if she were walking on quicksand. The more she struggled to break free, the deeper she was sucked in.

'Why is it that whenever we're together we seem to fight?' he said huskily.

She drew a deep breath. 'I don't know.'

'You seem to bring out the worst in me.' His fingers caressed the curve of her cheek. 'I came here expecting a quiet life, instead of which it's been like living on the edge of a volcano.'

'That not——' she opened her mouth to protest, but he silenced her, placing a finger against her lips.

'Why don't we call a truce?' He drew her towards him, slowly. His mouth moved over hers, then he raised his head long enough to look at her, a question glittering in his eyes.

She gasped at the shaft of exquisite pleasure his touch sent coursing through her. This was crazy. There was no future in it. She should put a stop to it now, before it was too late.

She shook her head, pushing weakly against him. 'Please, don't. We're not thinking rationally.'

He relaxed his grip to look at her with narrowed eyes. 'I don't need to think to know that I need you.'

But needing wasn't loving. Her hands pressed against his chest. 'I. . . I can't.'

He said thickly, 'You can't deny that you want me as much as I want you.'

She shook her head. It would have been pointless even to try to deny it. She stared at him. 'Paul needs me. He's asked me to marry him.'

His mouth tightened. 'You don't owe him anything, Thea. I admire your sense of loyalty, even if it is misguided. But isn't it time you started being honest with yourself?'

'I. . . I don't know what you mean.'

'Don't you?' Hot colour invaded her cheeks as he went on mercilessly. 'You don't love him, Thea. You couldn't respond to me as you just did, as you always do, if Prescott meant anything to you.'

'That's unfair.' His mocking reminder of those moments spent in his arms was like a blow.

'Shall I prove it to you, Thea?' His hand brushed against her cheek, his fingers tangling in her hair. 'I can, so easily.' His lips brushed against hers. 'What you feel for Prescott isn't love.'

'No,' she said weakly. She struggled to evade him, twisting her head away, but he brought her back again. 'You don't know that.' Denial was her only defence against this man. 'I care for Paul, very much.'

'Fool yourself if you like.' His dark eyes narrowed, 'But I know the truth, Thea, and so do you. You simply have to admit it.'

'No.' Tears burned at the back of her eyelids. She blinked them away, afraid to let him see, to guess how vulnerable she was. She loved Joel, but she would never admit it to this man who made no secret of the fact that, while he wanted her, that was as far as his commitment went. She would have to accept him on those terms and she wasn't sure that she could do that, not if it meant she had to share him and knowing he would never return her love.

She shook her head, an overwhelming desire for escape surging through her. 'You don't know Paul,' she said in a choked whisper. 'He's kind. He may have his faults but, basically, he's a caring man and I'm very fond of him.' She moved away from him, evading him when he would have held her.

'Fondness isn't enough basis for a marriage, Thea.'

'Maybe not,' she agreed. 'But at least it's something to work on. It's something we have in common.'

'Thea, wait.'

She shook his hand away. 'I'd like to go home.'

'We can talk. . .'

Her throat was very tight, making it hard for her to breathe. She said hoarsely, 'There's nothing to say. I think it would be better if we didn't see each other again.'

Better, maybe, but not easier, not when the only man who could ever truly mean anything in her life was standing only a breath away, dark hair falling over his forehead, wanting everything except the one thing she most wanted to give: her love.

CHAPTER ELEVEN

'THERE we are, then, Maggie. That's the animals fed and watered. They should be fine now, until young Jack Redmond pops over tomorrow.' Thea stepped out of her wellingtons before walking into the warm kitchen.

Maggie Pemberton sat at the well-scrubbed table, nursing a cup of tea. Her eyes filled with sudden tears and she fumbled for a hanky. 'I don't know how to thank you.'

'There's no need.' Thea hurried to sit beside her, taking the rough hand in hers. 'I was only doing my job; that's what vets get paid for.' She deliberately injected a note of humour into her voice. 'The important thing was to get you back on your feet again.'

'I'd never have managed on my own. I couldn't have left the animals if you and that nice Dr Forrester hadn't come along and taken care of everything.' She shoved the hanky into her pocket, smiling as the door edged open and a large black cat sidled in, brushing against her legs, purring loudly. She reached down to fondle his ears. 'You missed me, did you? Silly old cat.'

'They all did,' Thea said gently. 'I enjoyed having them. They're all real characters, aren't they?' She knew it was the right thing to say, as the older woman's face betrayed the first hint of a smile.

'Not everyone likes cats.'

'Well, they just happen to be a favourite of mine.'

Gratefully, Thea drank her own cup of tea while at the same time carefully assessing the way in which the other woman moved about the small kitchen. 'Oh, and by the way, we decided to keep one of the kittens at the surgery for a few days longer. It was much smaller than the rest of the litter, so we've been feeding her up a bit and giving her some extra vitamins, but I'll bring her over at the weekend if that's all right?' She glanced fondly at Maggie. 'The question now is, are you going to be able to cope?'

Maggie smiled. 'I'll be fine, my dear. Dr Forrester has taken care of everything. He's arranged for someone to come in every day, just to help out a bit, until I can manage again, and he says he'll be dropping by himself.' She laughed. 'To keep an eye on me, he says, but I reckon it's my clove and apple pie he's after. He's such a nice man. So like his uncle, don't you think so?'

Hastily, Thea rose to her feet. 'I'm sure you're right. Goodness——' forcing a smile, she glanced at her watch '—just look at the time. They'll be sending out a search party if I don't get a move on.' She reached for her bag. 'Now, you're sure you're going to be all right?'

'Bless you, I'll be fine.' Maggie followed her to the door, the cat at her heels. 'I know I've got to take things more easily. Dr Forrester warned me, I could end up back in hospital if I don't.' Her weather-lined face became serious. 'The nurses were all very kind, but I like to be outdoors. I can't abide central heating. I feel suffocated in those modern places.'

'I know what you mean,' Thea said. 'But you have to look after yourself, for the animals' sake. If you become ill, what will happen to them?'

'Now don't you worry. I've learned my lesson. I'll not do anything silly.' Maggie's surprisingly strong hand covered Thea's. 'You've been very kind, you and Dr Forrester. He was telling me about this idea of yours. Said it made a lot of sense.'

Thea frowned. 'Which idea was that?'

'Something about patting dogs.'

Thea laughed. 'Oh, you mean the Pat-a-Dog scheme.'

'Aye, that's the one. He reckons, as soon as it's arranged, he'd like me to go along with him, once a week, perhaps, to one of the hospitals or day-care centres. He thought we could take Rex along, for the old folk to make a fuss of.'

Thea struggled to hide a smile at the idea that Maggie thought of *other* people as old folk. 'I'm sure they'd love it,' she said warmly.

'Aye, and so would Rex. He's a soft old thing. Wouldn't hurt a fly.'

'Yes, well, that's obviously very important.'

'So you'll be coming with us, then?'

'Well. . . I — er — it's not really. . .'

'Dr Forrester reckoned as how, since it was your idea, you should be in on it.'

Oh, did he, indeed? 'Yes, well I'm afraid it will rather depend on how heavily I'm committed at the surgery,' she muttered evasively. Glancing up at the darkening clouds scudding across the sky, Thea turned up the collar of her jacket. 'We'll have to see,' she smiled. 'Anyway I must dash. Nial Frazer called the surgery to say a couple of his calves are coughing. It sounds as if they may have picked up a dose of husk. I'd better go and check before I head back.'

'He won't like that.' Maggie followed her to the gate. 'Not if it's going to cost him a penny or two. That man was born tight.'

Thea burst out laughing. 'I'm afraid it may well. Anyway, I'll pop in again, Maggie, and remember, don't overdo things. See you soon.'

The threatening rain actually gave way to sunshine about half an hour later, as she drove along the lanes where the hedges and trees thickened with late spring growth. It came through the car windows, striking warmly against her face and arms, and for the first time in days she began to relax.

Not that it could last, the thought came crowding in. Sooner or later she was bound to bump into Joel. A couple of days of careful avoidance had done nothing to lessen the tension, she admitted the fact ruefully. It was only postponing the inevitable. There was only one way to avoid him altogether and that was to get away completely.

The idea hit her with such force that, for a moment,

her attention was distracted from the road and she had to fight to bring her concentration back. To leave? Not just the job but the island? It had been her home for the past three years. She had made so many friends.

It was something she would dread doing, yet what was the alternative? To stay and see Joel, to know that he would always be there and have to pretend that nothing had happened? She knew it wouldn't be possible, not when the mere sight of him was enough to throw her normally well-controlled emotions into turmoil.

Driving past the small health centre, her gaze automatically registered Joel's small sports car, neatly parked where it always was, and, beside it, Helen Crawford's small blue Metro.

Thea was suddenly aware that her hands were gripping the steering-wheel too tightly. Gritting her teeth, she looked swiftly away, but a feeling of depression seemed to follow her all the way back to the surgery.

The rest of the morning sped by as she worked her way through an extremely busy surgery. Apart from the usual, routine canine injections against parvo virus and distemper, a large, elderly red setter limped into the treatment-room and promptly resisted every effort to trim a dew claw which had grown into the soft tissue of his leg.

'I think we're going to need a little help here,' Thea smiled at the anxious-looking woman who watched despairingly as her pet managed to wind his lead round the leg of the examination table.

'He hates having his nails clipped. He remembers the last time. Not that it hurt him. . .'

'Most dogs get a little nervous,' Thea offered the reassurance. 'You're a lovely old thing, aren't you?' she spoke soothingly to the nervous animal. Unfortunately this was quite a common problem in older animals. They tended to take less exercise so, obviously, the claws grew longer. Sometimes, in very bad cases, they could curl round and grow back into the foot. 'Let's have a look, shall we? It's all right, boy, I won't hurt you.'

Gently lifting each paw in turn, Thea inspected the pads. 'Yes, well, they're not too bad but they all need a trim. The dew claw, that's this small toe, here on the inside of the leg, is always more of a problem. You need to be sure it doesn't make contact with the ground otherwise it can become sore and infected.'

'I didn't like to cut his claws myself,' Mrs Rogers said anxiously. 'He's such a big dog and anyway I've heard they can bleed if you cut them too short.'

'Yes, that's true, they can bleed, and if you have a particularly energetic dog, it's probably easier to let your vet do the job. If you do accidentally cut the claw too short, though, the trick is not to panic. You can quite easily stem the bleeding by taking a bar of soap and drawing it across the claw. The soap impacts into the nail and shuts off the bleeding. But, right now,' she spoke softly, looking at the dog, 'we'd better sort out this particular old chap. You take his head. Hold him securely but talk to him, reassure him. Sandra, you deal with the business end and I'll sneak up on him and see if I can sort out this little problem before he knows what we're up to.'

Using a special pair of nail clippers, Thea cut each of the claws at a perpendicular angle to the axis of the nail, trimming to about a quarter of an inch outside the pink mark which identified the blood supply. The dew claws had actually penetrated the skin and she had to carefully extract the embedded tip of the nail.

'There we are,' she straightened up, smiling. 'You'll feel a lot happier now that that's out of the way, won't you old thing? Now, we'll just clean up the wound and put a small, anti-bacterial dressing on it to prevent any infection getting into it.'

'Will he need a tetanus injection?'

'Do you live in or near a farm, or anywhere where he's likely to come into contact with horse manure or stables or anything like that?' Mrs Rogers shook her

head. 'Well, in that case, I don't think we need to
worry,' Thea said. 'Dogs and cats are relatively resistant
to tetanus anyway, so it's not something you need to
worry too much about. There we are, all done.'

'Another satisfied customer.' Sandra grinned as she
disinfected the examination table. 'Ready for the next?'

They came in all shapes and sizes, from goldfish with
fungal infections, to budgies whose beaks needed trimming; from a pregnant hamster to a cat with
constipation.

'He sits in his litter box but he doesn't do anything,'
one anxious child explained, while her mother looked
on.

'That's right,' she said. 'He strains a lot, but Debbie's
right, nothing happens.'

'Let's take a look at him.' Thea placed the cat on the
table, making a careful examination. 'What's his appetite like?'

'Well he's been off his food for a few days, and he's
not at all his lively old self.'

Thea nodded. 'Cats do get constipated.' Even as she
said it, she was checking that there wasn't some kind of
urinary or pelvic obstruction. 'It often happens as they
get older.' She smiled. 'I'm sure there's nothing
seriously wrong. What sort of food does Cyril eat?'

The woman frowned. 'Funnily enough, we changed
to dried food a while ago. It seemed so much more
convenient, now that the weather is getting warmer. It
doesn't smell or go off.'

'It's very good,' Thea smiled. 'It has all the vitamins
and minerals a cat needs and, as you say, it is convenient. The one thing you need to be sure of though,
is that Cyril always has plenty of water to drink. You
could try soaking the food in water as well, that may
help. Perhaps if you tried giving him liver and milk,
once a week, and a vitamin B supplement. They all
help to prevent constipation, but never give a pet a
laxative on a regular basis. What you need to do now,'
she explained, 'is to give Cyril a mixture of milk of

magnesia and liquid paraffin. You can pick it up from the dispensary on your way out. I'm sure you'll find it will do the trick.'

Thea wrote up the notes on the card and handed it to the now smiling child. 'Cyril will be fine. He's a lovely cat. You must be very proud of him.'

An hour later the waiting-room was clear and Thea gratefully accepted a cup of coffee. 'I'd better pop through to see Andrew. I need a word about Maggie's kitten. I said I'd get it back to her as soon as possible but I don't want to rush it, or we'll be back to square one.'

'I'll finish up here.' Sandra collected the morning's cards. 'I'll pop these into Reception then go for lunch, if that's OK?'

'Fine, go ahead.' Thea smiled. 'I'll be away myself as soon as I've filled in a couple of forms.'

'It's your afternoon off, isn't it?'

'Mm, lovely thought.'

'In that case, enjoy it.' Sandra waved and Thea turned back to the treatment cards she had stacked into a neat pile. A whole afternoon off. At any other time she would have relished the thought, but right now, for some reason, the prospect seemed vaguely daunting.

She was writing up the last of her notes and checking the stock on the shelves when someone tapped at the door and it opened.

'Hi, am I intruding?'

'Joanne! No, of course not.' Thea smiled. 'Come in. Half an hour ago and you might have got killed in the rush but we've just finished. Take a seat. I'm almost finished here.'

Smiling, Joanne turned to Thea. 'I got your note by the way. Thanks.' She dropped, groaning, into a chair, easing one foot out of her shoe. 'Oh, my feet.'

'Shopping?' Thea grinned.

'How did you guess?' She massaged her toes. 'As a matter of fact, I was rather hoping to catch Andrew, but he doesn't seem to be around.'

'Ah, no. I was hoping for a word myself, but I gather he had to go out on a call.' Thea stacked books on to a shelf. 'Was it urgent.'

'No.' Joanne grinned. 'I was just hoping I might talk him into taking me to Lorenzo's for lunch and a rather nice bottle of wine, that's all.'

'Sounds nice.' Thea glanced at her, smiling. 'Still celebrating?'

'Actually—' a flush rose in the other girl's cheeks '—this is something different.' She looked at Thea and grinned. 'Oh heck, I have to tell someone or I'll burst. The thing is, I'm pregnant.'

Her own problems were temporarily forgotten as Thea leapt to embrace her friend. 'Oh, that's wonderful. I'm thrilled for you both.' She hesitated. 'I take it you are pleased?'

Joanne laughed. 'Delighted. I have to admit, it was a bit of a shock. It wasn't exactly planned.' She moved to half sit on the desk. 'Simon's almost ten. It's going to take some getting used to, all those nappies and disturbed nights again, but—' she smiled '—yes, I'm thrilled to bits.'

'I take it you haven't broken the good news to Andrew yet?'

'Not officially. I mean, we both guessed, but I went to the clinic this morning and it was confirmed. Hence the celebration lunch, but it doesn't matter. Heaven knows, we've got plenty of time.'

'When is the baby due?'

'October-ish.' Joanne chuckled. 'It's probably just as well, I got rid of all my baby stuff, so I'll have to start from scratch.'

Thea smiled. 'I should imagine that's half the fun, preparing for it, I mean.'

Joanne grinned. 'The down side is when none of my clothes fit. Look, I know it's early days, but we shall want you to be godmother.' She straightened up. 'At least we've got six months or so to come up with a name. All suggestions will be welcome, by the way.

Andrew and I almost came to blows when we were trying to decide for the boys.'

Thea was on her feet too now. 'I'm really touched that you should think of me,' she drew a deep breath, 'but. . .'

'Oh lor, you don't object do you? I mean, I know it's a huge responsibility and all that. . .'

'It isn't that.' Thea hesitated. 'The fact is. . .well, I'm not sure I'll still be here. The thing is, I've been thinking of making a move.'

Joanne stared at her. 'You're not serious?' She frowned. 'You *are* serious. But. . .why? I don't understand. It's not the job, is it? Something at the practice? Have you discussed it with Andrew? I'm sure he wouldn't want to lose you. If it's a matter of money. . .?'

'No, really. It's nothing like that.' Thea drew a hand shakily through her hair. 'I love the job and everything's fine at the practice.' She swallowed hard, unconsciously shifting objects on the desk, anything to keep her hands occupied. 'I just feel it's time I made a move,' she managed thickly. 'I've been thinking about it for a while.'

Joanne looked stunned. 'How does Paul feel about it?'

Thea's lips compressed as she swept a pile of cards up and said briskly, 'I haven't discussed it with him yet. As a matter of fact, he's taken a few days off. He was due a few days' leave, so he's gone to his sister to convalesce.'

Paul's fairly sudden departure had taken her by surprise. He had phoned briefly, late in the evening. 'I thought I'd take a couple of days off, get away somewhere.'

It was worrying to discover that her only reaction had been one almost of relief. In some respects it had helped to clear away a lot of confusion, making her see, far more clearly, that she didn't love Paul, probably never had. She was very fond of him, always would be.

But that wasn't a strong enough basis for marriage, she knew that now.

Joanne looked at her in troubled silence for a minute. 'I thought you and Paul had a. . .' She coloured slightly. 'That is — well, I mean. . .everyone thought. . .'

Thea gave a slight smile. 'That we were sort of unofficially engaged?' She shrugged. 'Maybe that's the trouble. It became a sort of habit and we went along with it. Oh, I'm not saying that we aren't good friends. . .'

'It's just not quite what everyone thought?'

'It took me a while to realise it.' And someone like Joel. Thea sighed. 'It wouldn't have worked out between Paul and me, I realise that now. In fact, I think I've known it for some time. I just didn't want to admit it to myself.' She raised her hands in a gesture of impotence. 'We both want. . .need very different things.'

'But surely you don't have to leave? You said yourself, you love it here. What will you do? Where will you go?'

Thea shook her head. 'I don't know. I haven't thought that far ahead. It's all still very muddled.'

'What about the refuge?'

Thea snapped the locks on her briefcase. 'That, at least, is out of my hands. The lease expires in about six months.'

'So, you renew it. What's wrong with that? It's never been a problem.'

'Not until now, maybe.' Thea hunted for her keys. 'In case you've forgotten, Bob doesn't own the land any more.'

'I still don't see the problem.' Joanne threw her a look. 'Talk to Joel.'

'I already have. It seems he has other plans.' She gave a slight smile. 'Land is a valuable commodity these days. I suppose I can't really blame him for wanting to sell.'

Joanne stared at her. 'Sell? Joel?' She gave a laugh

of incredulity. 'You're not serious? Whatever gave you that idea?'

Thea frowned. 'Joel himself, as it happens. I gather houses are a much more viable proposition these days.'

Joanne shook her head. 'No, I'm sure you must be mistaken. Joel's roots are here.'

'Maybe they were. People can change, grow away.'

Suddenly Joanne threw her a long, hard look. 'It's Joel, isn't it? That's what this is really all about? You've fallen for him.'

Thea ran a shaking hand through her hair. 'Oh lor, I hadn't realised it was so obvious.'

'It isn't. Put it down to my condition. They say pregnancy can heighten one's sense of awareness. Seriously, though, why not wait and reconsider. Things may work out.' She watched Thea brush a strand of hair from her eyes.

'It wouldn't work. Joel made it perfectly clear, right from the start, that I'm a thorn in his flesh and that, as far as he's concerned, the sooner I move out, the better. The feeling is entirely mutual, I might add.' She hoped her voice carried more conviction than she felt as she said it. 'Besides, it isn't only Joel.' She swallowed hard on the tightness in her throat. 'There are too many reasons why it's better if I go. Things can't go on as they are. Even if I could find somewhere else to keep the animals, I can't afford to pay a higher lease on top of the cost of feed and medicines, and I'm not prepared simply to abandon them.'

Joanne sighed. 'You know Andrew is going to be devastated. I wish you'd give yourself time. . .'

'Unfortunately that's a luxury I don't have.' Thea forced a smile. 'Andrew is a good vet. I shall miss him, and you and the children, but it's time I made a move. I need to widen my experience.' She forced a smile. 'Who knows? It may work out for the best. I may even set up a practice of my own one day.' She looked at her watch. 'I'd better go.' She paused at the door. 'Will you let me break the news to Andrew? I need to work a few things out first, get things straight in my own mind.'

But that was easier said than done, she thought, as she let herself into the cottage half an hour later. How, she wondered, staring out of the window, could life have become so complicated in so short a space of time? How could one man be responsible for such confusion? Without being aware of it she sighed and Jess came to nuzzle at her hand, gazing at her, wistfully.

'You're right.' She fondled the dog's ears. 'What we both need is a brisk walk and a dose of fresh air.' It might not solve her problems but at least it might help to get rid of her headache.

Minutes later, clad in a warm jacket, she was striding out in comfortable walking shoes, across the fields, looking for visible signs that summer wasn't too far away.

It was disheartening to visualise the countryside as it would be a few weeks from now, with sunlight cutting a path across the sea, holidaymakers thronging the nearby beaches, and the hedgerows bursting with new growth. She felt a sudden tightening in her chest at the realisation that she wouldn't be here to enjoy it.

It was a bright but chilly day, the wind bringing a glow to her cheeks and ruffling her hair, which she had purposely brushed loose from its customary restraining plait. She spent an hour throwing stones for a boisterous Jess, who bounded away and came back, panting and eager for more.

By the time she came within sight of the cottage half an hour later, her feeling of depression had lifted and she realised she was actually hungry.

'Come on, Jess.' Her pace quickened. She felt cold but refreshed and was actually enjoying a late lunch of hurriedly heated soup when someone tapped urgently at the door.

'Oh, no! Now who on earth can that be?' She flung the door open and felt the colour flood into her cheeks. 'You!'

'Don't close the door, Thea,' Joel's voice cut in tersely, his hand restraining her attempts to shut him out. 'I need to see you.'

'I thought I'd made it quite clear that we've said all there is to say. I don't want to see you. . .' She heard her own voice sounding strangely strangled.

His voice cut in sharply again. 'This isn't a social call. I need your help. It's Wellie; he's had some sort of relapse. It looks bad.'

'Where is he?' She was instantly all professional.

'In the car. I knew there was a risk in moving him, but I figured it would be quicker if I brought him to you?'

'You did the right thing.'

'I'll bring him in.'

She waited, standing back as he went to the car, lifting out a bundle wrapped in a blanket and hurried inside.

'Bring him through here.' She went ahead of him to the kitchen. 'Put him on the table.' She was already reaching for her briefcase, taking out a stethoscope. Wellie lay limp and unmoving. 'Tell me what happened.'

'He hardly touched his food yesterday but he seemed OK when I left him this morning. A bit sleepy maybe, reluctant to get out of his bed. It's not like him, he's usually so eager to go for a walk.'

Listening to the frail thud of the dog's heartbeat, Thea nodded. 'Any vomiting?'

'Slightly.' Joel looked at her. 'If you can fix him up, I don't care what it takes or what it costs. I take it you'll want to keep him here for a few days again, to keep an eye on him. . .'

'I don't think so.' Thea let the stethoscope fall..

'It's no trouble to bring a few of his things, his bed, feeding bowl.'

Thea swallowed hard. 'There's no point, Joel. He's gone.'

He stared at her. She saw the muscle in his jaw twitch.

'I'm sorry.' Her voice cracked. 'His heart just gave out. If it's any consolation, he wasn't in any pain. He was just old and very tired.' A sob caught in her throat as she stared at him, bleakly, then, before she knew what was happening, the tears were coursing down her cheeks and, with one gruff oath, he had taken her in his arms and was smoothing back her hair.

'It's all right, Thea, it's all right.'

'This is ridiculous,' she choked. 'He wasn't even my dog.' And she was a vet after all. It was a sad but inevitable fact that animals died. But it was more than that, she knew. It was a sudden releasing of a build-up of tensions. It was Wellie and Paul and this man who was cradling her head against his chest, surrounding her with his male presence and suddenly she was afraid, afraid but excited as well. He was too close, eating silently away at her resistance.

With a tiny gasp she drew away. Placing a blanket over Wellie, she fumbled for the switch on the electric kettle. 'I think we need some coffee.'

Joel's hand came down over hers, stilling her agitated movements as he turned her to face him. 'I don't need coffee, Thea.'

She willed him not to touch her, not to come any closer. Right now her resistance was at its lowest ebb. One hint of sympathy, one word and she just knew she would end up in his arms.

He didn't say a word. He bent towards her and his mouth found hers. His hand threaded into her hair as he drew back, his eyes held her gaze, seeming to question, seeing the momentary panic as his hand moved sensuously over her hips, upwards to the curve of her breast. She felt the colour flame into her cheeks.

'D-don't you think. . .?'

'You don't want to know what I'm thinking,' he told her.

There was no denying that, she thought, as he bent

his head again to kiss her, and she was incapable of
thinking of anything, except that she was in his arms
and it seemed right, as if her place had always been
there.

The pressure of his mouth was hard against hers and
she responded unashamedly and was drawn closer
against the strong, hard masculinity of him, and when
he released her briefly she heard herself murmur,
'Don't leave me.'

'Don't worry, Thea, I don't intend to.' His voice was
hoarse as his mouth claimed hers again and she felt
herself being lifted and carried through to the sitting
room.

He set her down on the sofa. Her hands moved up to
his neck and his arms tightened like a steel band around
her and she heard her own swift gasp of shock as the
contact renewed the fire that seemed to be coursing
through her, burning out of control.

'Thea,' he groaned softly, feathering kisses over her
throat, chin, eyes before claiming her mouth again.

'This shouldn't be happening,' she said weakly.

'Don't fight it, Thea, don't try to understand. Just let
it happen.'

He was right. This was crazy, utterly crazy. But she
would think about that later, much later. She moved
beneath him, suddenly more sure than she had ever
been of anything in her life.

The sound of the phone ringing brought her, shaking,
back to reality.

'Let it ring.' Joel's lips drew her own back but, with
the strident ringing, common sense returned and she
pushed him gently away, trying to steady her breathing.

'I can't,' she groaned. 'I'm on call. It might be
urgent.'

'This is urgent,' he groaned as she groped for the
phone, fumbling with the receiver as he nibbled at her
ear until she tilted her head away and said breathlessly,
'Yes. Thea Somers.'

Paul's voice sounded anxious, awkward. 'Hello, Thea, darling. I'm sorry it's late but I just got back.'

'Paul.' Her voice seemed to be trapped somewhere in her throat as Joel looked at her and slowly began to get to his feet, his face a frozen mask. The laughter slid from her eyes, taking with it some of the giddy sense of elation. She wanted to draw him back, to regain the moment.

'I just called to check that you're OK and still want to meet tomorrow, as usual.'

'Tomorrow?' She was on her feet too, now, her head spinning as she tried to think. She reached out a hand as Joel looked at her and slowly began to move towards the door.

'Don't worry, Thea,' he said quietly. 'I'll see myself out and don't worry. I understand. I promise I won't bother you again.'

He was gone before she could say another word and she was left, staring blankly at the door as it closed behind him, scarcely aware of anything as Paul's voice continued speaking in her ear.

CHAPTER TWELVE

'WHY DON'T you give yourself a bit of space? At least take some time off to think about it.' Andrew tapped the stem of his empty pipe against his hand as he eased himself upright from where he had been half sitting, half standing against the desk. 'You know, don't you, that I shall be damn sorry to see you go?'

Thea's throat tightened painfully as she dragged her gaze briefly from the rain-lashed street below, and the small harbour which was shrouded in low cloud. 'I know, and I appreciate the vote of confidence, really.'

'But you won't reconsider?'

She turned slowly, her arms wrapped around her body in a kind of self-protective embrace. 'I can't.' She forced a smile. 'It's time I moved on. I've settled into a nice, comfortable rut here.'

'Nothing wrong with that,' he said evenly. 'There's a lot to be said for stability. People find it reassuring. They like to see the same faces.'

Thea swallowed hard. 'You're not making this easy, you know?'

'Good.' Andrew sucked at the still unlit pipe, frowning as he ran a hand through his hair. 'So, what will you do?'

'I haven't decided. I'm thinking of joining a practice where I can perhaps expand my work with the refuge side of things. I enjoy that aspect of the work.' She dug her hands into the pockets of her jeans. 'In time I may devote myself solely to rescue work. You know yourself, there's certainly a need for it.'

'And when exactly are you thinking of going?'

'As soon as possible.'

Andrew nodded. 'You certainly seem to have thought things out.'

Nothing could be further from the truth, Thea thought. She was running scared. Scared every day of seeing Joel, scared of her own reaction if she did. 'I realise you'll need time to advertise for a new partner.'

'But you won't change your mind?'

She shook her head. 'There's no point. In any case, as I explained to Joanne, the lease on the land runs out soon and I need to find an alternative site.' She forced a laugh. 'Apart from that there's also the small consideration of where I'm going to live.' She was aware of Andrew tensing as he moved towards the chair.

'Look, I don't want to interfere, but don't you think you may be over-reacting?' he said quietly. 'I mean, I know you and Joel haven't exactly seen eye to eye, but couldn't you come to some sort of compromise?'

She sighed, resisting the urge to probe at the dull ache in her temple as she turned to face him. 'It wouldn't work. Things are never that simple. I need a change, to get away.'

'You know we're all going to miss you?'

'I shall miss you too. I've been very happy here.' But that was before, when her life had revolved around her work and Paul.

It was odd now to think that she could even have contemplated marrying him, that she had been content to let herself drift into it, until Joel had come along and turned her life upside down.

Paul's sudden departure, a few days ago, had only been part of it. It was inevitable, of course, she had sensed it for some time. Even so, the speed with which it had happened had shocked her.

Her thoughts flew back to their last meeting when she had told Paul, quite calmly, that she didn't love him and couldn't marry him. She had waited, steeling herself for the arguments, but they hadn't come. Instead, the calmness with which he had accepted it had shaken her.

He had looked at her then said simply, 'I suppose I've seen it coming. We both have, haven't we?' He had smiled slightly and brushed a hand against her cheek. 'It might have worked out, but we'll never know, will we, Thea?'

'We both want different things.'

'It's Forrester, isn't it?'

Shocked, she had tried to deny it. She hadn't seen or heard from Joel since that night. If he was deliberately trying to avoid her then he was succeeding admirably.

A few days later she heard that Paul had gone. She had waited for the feelings of regret, for a sense of loss to settle in. But it hadn't. That had told her, more clearly than anything, that she had been right to end it.

All she needed now was a fresh start, somewhere where the memories wouldn't haunt her, so that, eventually, there might even come a day when, even if she couldn't entirely forget Joel, she would be able to think of him without that awful feeling of pain in her heart.

She looked directly at Andrew and forced a smile. 'I've loved every minute I've worked with you. I love Joanne and the boys, but it's time I spread my wings, learned to fly on my own. Maybe, some day, I'll have my own practice. You've given me the confidence to do that. Don't spoil it,' she said gently.

His brows winged together in an expression of resigned disappointment. 'Well, at least if you change your mind, you know you'll always be welcome here.'

But as she made her way out to the car, Thea knew there was no chance of that, not as long as Joel was around.

In a way it was a relief to be kept so busy over the next few days that she scarcely had any time to think. The weather deteriorated with a vengeance. Trekking her way across muddy farmyards and tracks, it was late by the time she got back, tired and wet, to the cottage where, having seen all the animals secured, fed and watered, she heated a casserole and ate it in front of a roaring fire, listening with the first real stirrings of anxiety to the strengthening wind outside.

Jess nuzzled closer, her head on Thea's feet and she shivered. 'You're right. It's no night to be out.' Sparing a thought for Andrew who was on emergency call, she gave in to a stab of concern, threw a jacket over her shoulders and, taking a flashlight, made a second check on the outhouse and cages. The animals seemed restless, as if their instincts were alerting them to an impending storm.

Back in the kitchen once more, she made herself a cup of hot chocolate, locked the doors and checked the windows. 'Sleep tight, Jess,' she murmured, as the collie settled in her basket, 'though I can't help feeling we're all in for a restless night.'

In the bedroom, later, a towelling robe over her nightie, she walked to the window and stared out into the darkness. Through the movement of the trees she could distinguish a light, coming from the direction of Joel's cottage. A glance at the clock showed midnight. Perhaps the storm was keeping him awake too.

Yawning, she tore herself away and climbed into bed. She had to be up early in the morning. Which made it all the more galling to discover that when she pulled the covers over her head an image of Joel rose to haunt her.

'Go away!' She sat up, plumping the pillows crossly with her fist and closing her eyes firmly. But not firmly enough to shut him out of her thoughts completely.

Tomorrow she would start job-hunting in earnest. The sooner she got away from here, the sooner she could get her life together.

The more she thought about it, the more the irony of the situation struck her. She hadn't wanted to break the ties she had made in order to go away with Paul. But wasn't that precisely what she was planning to do now?

The phrase 'chickening out' sprang uncomfortably to mind. She pulled the sheet over her head, drawing a deep breath. At least she didn't fool herself she would be missed, not with Helen Crawford on hand, ready and willing to fill the gap.

Perhaps if she tried counting sheep? Somewhere a gate rattled. The wind made eerie sounds, like angry sighs. Two o'clock! Groaning, she turned over, burying her head in the pillow to shut out the sound of rain lashing against the window.

Gradually her numbed senses were lulled into an exhausted sleep, to be punctuated by dreams in which Paul herded sheep through gates and someone was demanding, angrily, that she wake up.

Except that it wasn't a dream. Someone was shaking her mercilessly. She woke, breathless and shaking, fighting the relentless, bruising hands that gripped her shoulders.

'Get up, damn you! Open your eyes.'

'Go away,' she groaned, fumbling for the covers. 'I need my sleep.'

'Oh, no, you don't. Wake up, damn it.'

Gradually she managed to force her sleep-drugged eyes open, gasping as Joel towered above her, his expression grim, his dark hair slicked back as if he had just stepped out of a shower.

He wasn't real, she told herself. It was all part of the dream, except that there was nothing in the least dreamlike about the hands which were shaking her until her teeth rattled.

'Wake up,' he demanded, relentlessly.

She sat up in the bed, wide-eyed and fully awake now. 'What are you *doing*? she demanded. She stared at him, realisation only now beginning to infiltrate her befuddled senses. Her glance flew to the bedside clock. '*Four o'clock*! It's still dark!' She scrabbled furiously for the sheet, drawing it up to her chin. 'This is my house, my bedroom,' she snapped. 'How did you get in? What do you want?' She wrenched the sheet out of his grasp. 'Don't you believe in knocking before you force your way in?'

The sardonic gaze narrowed briefly as he viewed her bare shoulders. 'Lady, believe me, right now your virtue is the last thing on my mind. As for knocking,

I've been hammering at the door for the past ten minutes. I don't know what you're on,' he gritted, 'but it must be pretty powerful stuff if you can sleep through what's going on out there.'

'On!' She glared at him. How dared he imply that she was some kind of druggy? 'You're crazy,' she snapped. 'Get out of here or do I have to——?'

'I don't have time to argue, Thea.'

She gasped as he dragged the covers unceremoniously off her. 'Get dressed,' he said curtly. 'Jeans, sweater, anything warm.'

'No way! I need my sleep. . .'

He wasn't even listening to her. He walked to the wardrobe, flinging open the doors, then tossed a pair of boots on to the bed. 'You'll need these. I take it you've got a torch?'

She struggled into her dressing-gown, securing the belt firmly before she stood up, conscious of him watching her every move. Her mouth was dry, she felt awful and probably looked worse.

'You don't seriously imagine I'm going anywhere with you. . .?'

'This isn't a game, Thea,' he advised hardly from the doorway. 'God knows how anyone could sleep through the racket that's going on out there. There's a tree down.'

Her voice was still thick with sleep. 'So what do you want me to do? Move it?' She was still battling with the realisation that he had been in her room, watching her sleep, and the idea was unnerving.

She was unprepared for the sudden tightening of his face as he breathed angrily, 'It's come down on one of the fences and part of the outbuildings. Your animals are running riot, some might be injured for all I know.'

Her face paled. 'Oh, God. . . Look, I'm sorry.'

'Just get dressed.' He stalked out of the room, leaving her to stare after him in confusion.

Minutes later, washed, having pulled on jeans and a sweater, raking her fingers through her hair, she raced downstairs to find him in the kitchen, pouring boiling water into mugs of instant coffee.

He handed her a mug. 'You'd better drink this.'

'I want to see what damage has been done,' she said tightly. 'The animals may be hurt.' She started towards the peg where her jacket hung.

'I said drink this first. It's freezing out there. It's also wet and dark. Besides which,' his mouth hardened, 'I've just taken a cursory look round. As far as I can tell there's structural damage to the building but the animals seem OK. You were damn lucky.'

'*Lucky!*' He might think so. She almost choked on the coffee, wincing as the strong black liquid burned her throat. 'Some of those animals won't last the night, out there on their own. They weren't ready yet to be released back into the wild.' She stared at him in mute appeal, putting the mug on the table. 'I have to see for myself.'

He followed, saying nothing as she shrugged herself into her jacket and they went out to the paddock. He was right about the cold. She sucked in her breath, ducking her head, gasping as rain lashed into her face, taking her breath away.

The first rays of light were just beginning to appear in the distant sky. She was conscious of Joel beside her, the torch directing her footsteps, his hand firmly gripping her elbow when she would have stumbled.

They rounded the cottage. The beam of light from the torch flickered and she gasped at the sight of the large oak which lay, its roots unearthed. Its branches had missed the cottage, the very room where she had slept, by a matter of feet.

She shivered violently. Only now did she fully appreciate what he meant when he said she had been lucky. A few yards more and she might have been killed. Taking several deep breaths she half-turned away and came up against Joel's solid frame.

'Are you all right?'

She looked up, her face taut with strain, to find him

watching her, his lips set in a hard, fierce line. She
swallowed hard.

'I'm fine. I must check the animals.'

'Let me do it. It's still dangerous in there. We don't
know how much damage there is. . .'

She shook her head. 'They'll be frightened enough.
They know me. Just bring the torch.'

He was right about the damage. Picking her way
unsteadily through the debris of fallen slates and
branches, she realised, with gradually increasing
horror, that it was far worse than she had dared
imagine.

One side of the outbuilding had been almost totally
demolished by the falling tree. Several of the cages,
obviously caught by heavier branches, had fallen and
broken open. Going to each of the others in turn, she
did a quick mental survey and experienced a small stab
of relief.

'It's not as bad as it might have been. You were right,
at least there don't appear to be any injuries.'

'Here, let me do that,' Joel intervened, righting the
fallen cages as she went from one to the other, murmur-
ing soothingly to the terrified occupants.

'Can you tell what's missing?'

She straightened up, running a shaky hand through
her wet hair. 'It could have been a lot worse. As far as
I can tell, Gerald is the only one that's actually missing.'

His mouth twisted. 'Not Gerald again? Have you
ever considered renaming him Houdini?'

'He won't have gone far,' she muttered. 'In fact. . .'
Her eyes caught a sudden, small movement in a heap
of straw. 'Hand me that small cage.'

Moving slowly and quietly, she approached the
frightened animal. 'Come on, Gerald. Believe me, it's
no night to be running loose out there.'

'You can say that again,' Joel muttered.

She shot him a look, knelt down, manoeuvring the
cage and gave a small grunt of satisfaction as Gerald
was placed, unprotesting, inside.

Brushing a damp tendril of hair back from her cheek, Thea reached for the next of the cages which was lying at an angle. A small green parakeet with a damaged foot screeched in terror, flapping wildly.

'Let me take it.'

Joel took the cage she handed to him and she drew a sharp breath as she saw a tiny rivulet of blood coursing down his hand.

'You're hurt.' Instinctively she reached out to inspect the wound. 'It's a pretty deep cut. It needs attention.'

'I'll live,' he grunted. 'Is there anything more we can do here?' And when she shook her head, 'In that case I'll anchor this tarpaulin. It should help to keep out the worst of the wind, then I suggest we get out of this rain. We'll go over to my place.'

'No, I. . .'

'I don't intend arguing, Thea,' he said grimly. 'I'm wet, cold and tired. Apart from that, once it's daylight we can get a proper assessment of the damage. Until then, there are more trees which could come down at any minute, in any direction. I'm not prepared to take the risk of you going back to that cottage.'

She knew it made sense and yet, standing, five minutes later, shivering, dripping water on to his thick, pale carpets, she wasn't at all sure she wouldn't rather have taken her chances with the elements.

He tossed a log on to the fire, sending a shower of sparks hurtling up the chimney before picking up the phone. 'At least this is still working. I was afraid the lines might be down. It's too early to call anyone yet.' His mouth was tight as he looked at her. 'You'd better get out of those wet things. You'll find jeans and sweaters upstairs. You may have to improvise. Help yourself to a shower, too; it'll help to warm you up. By the time you come downstairs I'll have some breakfast on the go.'

She felt the colour rising in her frozen cheeks. The mere thought of wearing his clothes, using his shower, bespoke an intimacy she dared not even begin to contemplate. Maybe it was also a measure of his indifference, that he should suggest it? the depressing thought hovered.

'I'm not hungry.' For some reason she couldn't stop shaking. 'I'll wait until I can get over to my own place, at least to pick up some of my things. It should be light in about half an hour. I can. . .'

'I'm afraid I can't allow that,' Joel said shortly.

Thea stared mutinously at him. 'Not allow. . .?'

'I happen to be the landlord,' he frowned, his dark brows drawing together in a dark line. 'I have no intention of being held responsible if the roof caves in while you're in there. Apart from which,' he silenced her attempt at protest, 'I refuse to take the blame when you go down with a dose of double pneumonia.'

'Oh, come on, not squeamish, surely?' she snapped, totally illogically. 'You must be delighted at the prospect of having me out of your hair once and for all. It's what you wanted.'

'If only it were that simple,' he gritted, drying his own hair with a towel. He tossed it aside and Thea gasped as he stripped off his sweater, revealing his tautly muscled chest.

Flickering firelight cast shadows, emphasising the wonderful planes of his face, drawing her gaze to the wide shoulders and tanned torso, the sensuous mouth and dark eyes which seemed to be having a strangely hypnotic effect.

He gave her own sweater a disparaging glance. 'At least take that off,' he said, tersely. 'It's soaked through. I'll find you something to put on.'

He disappeared upstairs. Thea stared down at her sweater, appalled to see how it clung to her figure. Hastily stripping it off, she jumped as Joel's voice sounded from behind her.

'Here, it's bound to be too big, but at least it's dry.'

She took it, struggling into it, her fingers numb with cold, losing her way among the heavy folds. She heard him swear softly, then froze as he pulled the thick sweater down over her head.

His arm brushed against her, setting her heart thudding. 'Th-thank you.' She tried to move but his hands were on her shoulders. She shivered in spite of the heat suddenly burning in her cheeks and tried to turn away.

His own breathing was ragged as he held her, turning her roughly towards him. His face was drawn into a frown and she could sense the sudden tension in him as his hand cupped her chin, forcing her to look into the compelling, blue eyes.

'Dammit. Why do I get the feeling that, wherever you are, somehow, you're still going to cause havoc in my life?' he ground out. 'What the hell is this about you leaving anyway? Andrew told me.'

'You can't have forgotten?' The words came out thickly through the constriction in her throat. 'My lease is almost up. I certainly can't afford to pay more rent. . .'

His gaze narrowed. 'I haven't said what I'm prepared to charge.'

'Whatever it is, I can't afford it.' She tried to free herself but his hands on her arms stopped her. 'Besides, you made it quite clear that you had other plans.'

'Plans can be changed.' His expression was harsh, the dark eyes glittering. 'Nothing was definite.'

She frowned at his anger. What was it he wanted? Why was she letting this happen? It seemed she only had to be near him for her emotions to run riot. It left her confused, emotionally drained, when what she needed more than anything right now was to be able to think clearly.

Her hands pushed against the taut, muscular warmth of his chest. 'There's no point discussing it. Don't you see?' Weakly she shook her head. 'What happened tonight only proves what we've both always known. We can't live as neighbours. It wouldn't work.' It *couldn't* work, because, no matter how hard she tried, she would never come to terms with her feelings for him. She loved him, but there was no way he would ever return her love. A casual relationship, yes, but, for the sake of her own sanity, she knew that she couldn't settle for that.

'So you're going to inflict the escapee rat on some other poor, unsuspecting soul?'

The hint of laughter in his voice infuriated her. How could he joke at a time like this? She pulled away, putting what seemed like a safe distance between them.

'You're a cold-blooded swine,' she advised him hardly.

His gaze narrowed. 'What's the matter, Thea? Got out of bed the wrong side? Well, there's a remedy for that.' His voice was deep and gritty. A brief and tantalising image of their previous intimacy rose to haunt her and she sucked in her breath audibly as he came, slowly, towards her. 'Or maybe you're missing the boyfriend? Well, there's a remedy for that too.'

Without warning, his hand slid round her waist, drawing her towards him. His mouth came down on hers, relentless, firm, demanding.

She told herself it was because he had caught her off guard that she experienced a sensation of exquisite longing. He raised his head to stare down at her. 'I'm sure we can come to some. . .mutual arrangement, about the lease, if that's what you want? As for the rest. . .'

She gasped. She couldn't believe she had heard the words. There was a taunting quality to his voice and she felt her knuckles tighten. 'Paul has nothing to do with it. If you must know, he's been offered a job, somewhere where he'll be appreciated. As for. . .'

'Is that what's making you so edgy?' Joel's gaze narrowed. 'You're angry because he couldn't wait to head for the bright lights? Is that why you're packing up? You can't wait to follow? You miss him warming your bed?'

She said stiffly, 'Paul and I parted on perfectly amicable terms, no thanks to you. And, as it happens,

there was never any question of my going with him, or
of. . .' She broke off, her eyes widening with shock at
the sudden gleam of triumph in his face. What had she
done? What had she said? Too late she realised he had
deliberately taunted her to make her drop her guard
and, like an idiot, she had fallen for it.

She threw him a hostile look. 'Your ego is showing,
Doctor. There's only one reason I'm leaving. . .'

His expression was brooding, his eyes very dark. 'It's
still not too late, Thea.'

'Too late?' she echoed.

'To go after him, if that's what you want?' He had
moved closer, his fingers absently tracing the pulse in
her wrist. '*Is* that what you want?' His sensuous mouth
was just a breath away. She closed her eyes, gritting
her teeth. 'Look at me, Thea. Look at me.'

She opened her eyes and wished she hadn't. Groaning softly she tried to turn her head away, only to feel
his hands cup her face, forcing her to look at him.

'I. . .no,' she almost sobbed in defeat, then anger
surfaced like a bright new weapon. 'Are you satisfied?'
she demanded. 'You said it wouldn't work, that Paul
wasn't right for me; well, you've been proved right.
You must be feeling very happy, Dr Forrester.'

His jaw tensed. 'I didn't have to prove anything. The
truth was there all the time; you just needed to see it.'

'You never did like Paul, did you?' she accused.
'From the moment you arrived, you decided to make
his life unbearable so that he would want to leave.'

'I didn't have to do that. As for liking him——' his
voice was suddenly rough-edged '—I didn't like seeing
him with you.'

She stared at him, feeling her breath catch in her
throat. 'Why should it matter? Why should you care?'

His brooding gaze narrowed. 'I told myself it
shouldn't, but it did.' His hand cupped her face, his
thumb tracing the generous curve of her mouth. He
said, 'The last thing I needed was any kind of compli-
cation in my life then, suddenly, there you were. You

and those damned animals. It was. . .as if someone had taken me by the scruff of the neck. . .' He broke off, raking a hand through his hair. 'One minute everything was under control, then I made the big mistake of kissing you and. . . I may have been wrong, but I sensed that you felt it too. Something——' he stared down at her '—something happened. I told myself it was crazy, but then. . .'

She stared at him, holding her breath. 'I don't understand. What are you trying to say?'

'That I was jealous,' he said, thickly. 'I told myself I didn't care, I wasn't interested. But the thought of the two of you, together, was driving me insane. I wanted you and I knew I couldn't be imagining the way you responded each time you were in my arms, and yet you seemed set on throwing yourself away. Have you any idea of the kind of hell I've been going through since I met you?'

She stared at him in silence, too afraid to try to put any interpretation on his words in case it might be wrong. Hesitantly she said, 'But, you didn't want any kind of commitment. Why should you care?'

His jaw tensed. 'I don't pretend there's any kind of logic to it. I wasn't even sure I was getting the right signals.' Her eyes widened and he said, impatiently, 'You made it quite clear there was nothing about me that you could like and yet——' he drew her closer, his eyes searching her face intently '—when I kissed you and you responded. . .' He drew her roughly back when she would have pulled away. 'When you responded, I knew I couldn't be mistaken. There was something there.'

His hands moved, tracing the soft, full curves of her breasts. A groan rose from deep in his throat. His arms tightened round her, as if he was afraid she might slip away. 'Shall I prove it to you, Thea?' He kissed her fiercely, hungrily.

'This isn't fair,' she complained, breathlessly. 'I still don't understand.'

Briefly his head rose and she saw the faint gleam in his eyes. 'I thought it must be perfectly obvious.'

'Not to me,' Thea made a small, explosive sound. 'What about Helen? Or have you conveniently forgotten that she exists, until it suits you to remember?'

'Helen means nothing to me,' Joel insisted flatly. 'At least, not in the way you seem to mean.'

'How can you say that?'

'Quite easily.' His fingers began their exquisite torment all over again. 'Because it just happens to be true. Helen and I practically grew up together. We've always been very good, close friends.'

'Hah!'

His shuddering breath whispered against her throat, her cheek, against her hair. 'Do I take it that you could be just a little jealous, Thea?' With a low growl, his mouth covered hers, silencing her denial. His hands were beneath the sweater, warm against the trembling silkiness of her skin and he groaned. 'Oh, Thea, I lose control whenever I'm near you. Have you any idea how much I want you, have wanted you since the first moment I set eyes on you?'

His mouth made a teasing foray, driving her to distraction. He kissed her again, fiercely, before raising his head. 'Helen is part of the past,' he breathed. 'I think she may have hoped for more, especially when I came back.'

'Your marriage,' she said softly. 'I heard. . .'

'Anyone can make a mistake. I'm not dismissing it, Thea. I thought it was going to last forever. I was wrong.' He looked down at her. 'For a while I told myself I'd never let it happen again, but then I hadn't counted on meeting an irresistible force like you, and when I did. . .all I could see was you, in Paul's arms.'

She drew a long, shaky breath. 'I don't love Paul. Oh, I may have thought I did, for a while, but it would never have worked. We wanted different things.'

'And I wanted you.'

She stared at him. 'But you wanted to get rid of me. You threatened to sell the land, to build. . .'

'I don't believe I ever quite said that,' he growled softly, and she saw the sudden, mischievous gleam in his eyes. 'I will admit, the lease was a weapon I used, to try to keep you here, but it damn nearly blew up in my face. It was the one means I had to stop you threatening to hand over to Andrew. Then, when I threatened not to let you renew and you suddenly called my bluff, I suddenly realised I might lose you anyway.' His voice roughened. 'I've never wanted anything, anyone, as much as I want you.'

The words were muffled as he bent his head, his mouth drifting warmly over her cheek. 'I love you, Thea. Say it,' he urged. 'Say that you love me.'

'I love you,' she whispered. 'I do love you. Oh, but —' her head jerked '—how am I going to explain to Andrew?'

'I don't think you'll need to explain. Anyone with eyes must see how much I need you.'

He kissed her again and Thea lifted a trembling hand to his face, gently stroking the wonderful planes of his features.

'Are you sure you know what you're taking on?' she whispered. 'It's not just me.'

'Don't tell me,' he muttered, trailing kisses over her eyes and mouth. 'Gerald's part of the deal too?'

'I'm afraid so,' she laughed softly.

'Why couldn't you have been a doctor instead of a vet?'

'Because that would have been too easy.' She nuzzled his ear, heard him mutter an oath under his breath. 'I do love you.'

He drew a long, shuddering breath as he looked into her eyes. 'Oh, well, I suppose we can always build an ark.'

'Later.' She gave a tremulous sigh.

'We'd better get married straight away,' he mumbled,